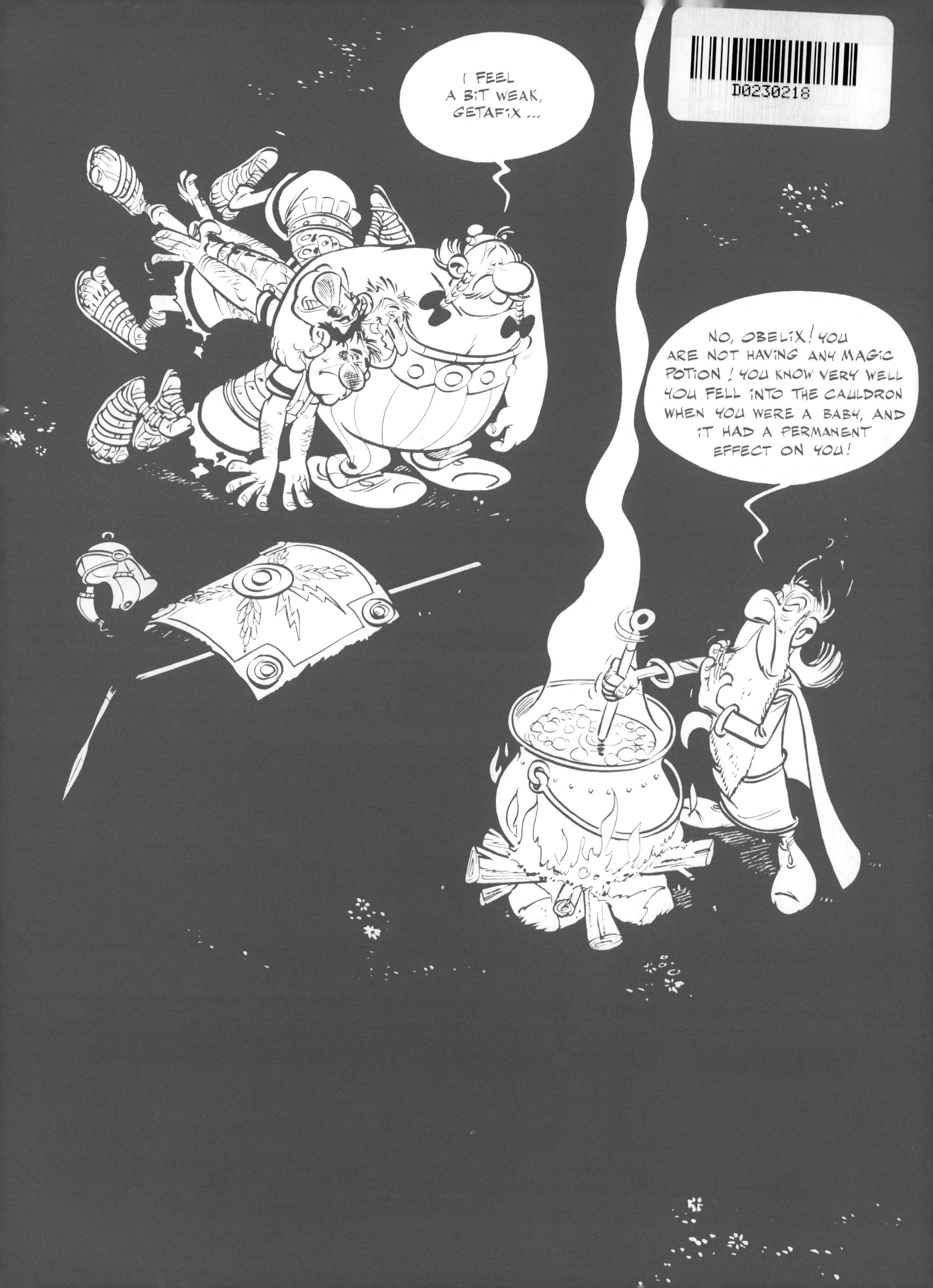
I FEEL A BIT WEAK, GETAFIX ...
NO, OBELIX! YOU ARE NOT HAVING ANY MAGIC POTION! YOU KNOW VERY WELL YOU FELL INTO THE CAULDRON WHEN YOU WERE A BABY, AND IT HAD A PERMANENT EFFECT ON YOU!
D0230218

GOSCINNY AND UDERZO

PRESENT

An Asterix Adventure

ASTERIX
AND SON

Asterix titles available now

1 Asterix the Gaul
2 Asterix and the Golden Sickle
3 Asterix and the Goths
4 Asterix the Gladiator
5 Asterix and the Banquet
6 Asterix and Cleopatra
7 Asterix and the Big Fight
8 Asterix in Britain
9 Asterix and the Normans
10 Asterix the Legionary
11 Asterix and the Chieftain's Shield
12 Asterix at the Olympic Games
13 Asterix and the Cauldron
14 Asterix in Spain
15 Asterixand the Roman Agent
16 Asterix in Switzerland
17 The Mansions of the Gods
18 Asterix and the Laurel Wreath
19 Asterix and the Soothsayer
20 Asterix in Corsica
21 Asterix and the Caesar's Gift
22 Asterix and the Great Crossing
23 Obelix and Co.
24 Asterix in Belgium
25 Asterix and the Great Divide
26 Asterix and the Black Gold
27 Asterix and Son
28 Asterix and the Magic Carpet
29 Asterix and the Secret Weapon
30 Asterix and Obelix All at Sea
31 Asterix and the Actress
32 Asterix and the Class Act
33 Asterix and the Falling Sky

Coming soon

Asterix versus Caesar
The Twelve Tasks of Asterix
Asterix Conquers America
Operation Getafix

Original title: *Le Fils d'Astérix*

10

Exclusive licensee: Orion Publishing Group
Translators: Anthea Bell and Derek Hockridge
Typography: Bryony Newhouse

First published in Great Britain in 1983 by Hodder Headline plc

This edition first published in Great Britain in 2001 by Orion Books Ltd,
Orion House, 5 Upper Saint Martin's Lane, London WC2H 9EA

Printed in France by Partenaires

http://gb.asterix.com
www.orionbooks.co.uk

A CIP record for this book is available from the British Library

ISBN-13 978 0 75284 714 6 (cased)
ISBN-10 0 75284 714 7 (cased)
ISBN-13 978 0 75284 775 7 (paperback)
ISBN-10 0 75284 775 9 (paperback)

Distributed in the United States of America by Sterling Publishing Co. Inc.
387 Park Avenue South, New York, NY 10016

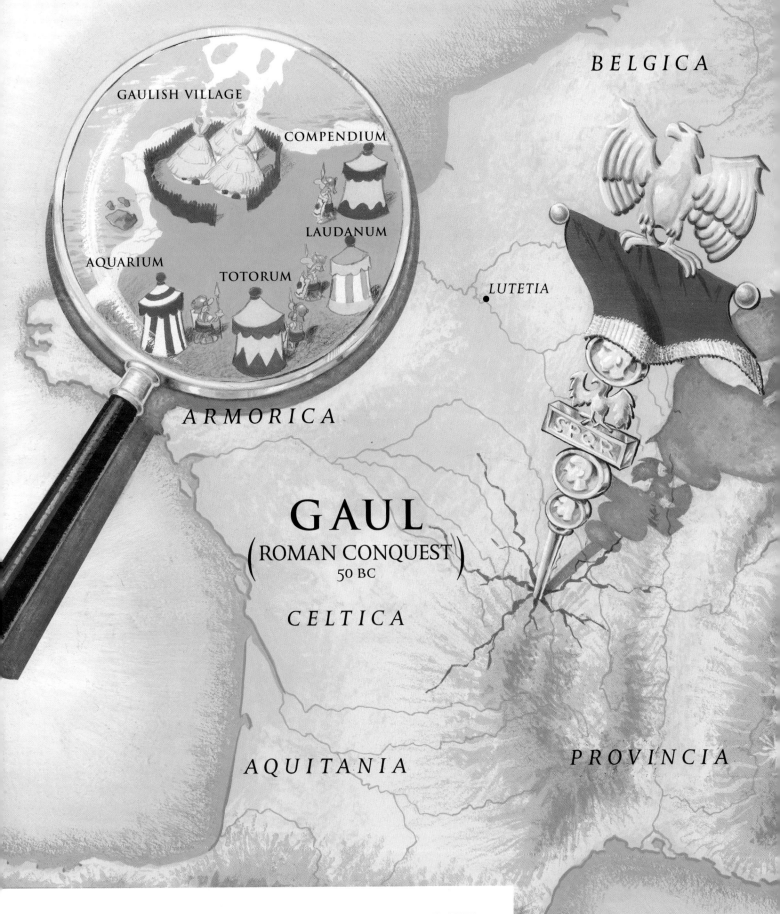

GAUL
(ROMAN CONQUEST)
50 BC

BELGICA

LUTETIA

ARMORICA

CELTICA

AQUITANIA

PROVINCIA

GAULISH VILLAGE

COMPENDIUM

LAUDANUM

AQUARIUM

TOTORUM

THE YEAR IS 50 BC. GAUL IS ENTIRELY OCCUPIED BY THE
ROMANS. WELL, NOT ENTIRELY . . . ONE SMALL VILLAGE OF
THE INDOMITABLE GAULS STILL HOLDS OUT AGAINST THE
INVADERS. AND LIFE IS NOT EASY FOR THE ROMAN LEGION-
ARIES WHO GARRISON THE FORTIFIED CAMPS OF TOTORUM,
AQUARIUM, LAUDANUM AND COMPENDIUM . . .

ASTERIX, THE HERO OF THESE ADVENTURES. A SHREWD, CUNNING LITTLE WARRIOR, ALL PERILOUS MISSIONS ARE IMMEDIATELY ENTRUSTED TO HIM. ASTERIX GETS HIS SUPERHUMAN STRENGTH FROM THE MAGIC POTION BREWED BY THE DRUID GETAFIX . . .

OBELIX, ASTERIX'S INSEPARABLE FRIEND. A MENHIR DELIVERY-MAN BY TRADE, ADDICTED TO WILD BOAR. OBELIX IS ALWAYS READY TO DROP EVERYTHING AND GO OFF ON A NEW ADVENTURE WITH ASTERIX – SO LONG AS THERE'S WILD BOAR TO EAT, AND PLENTY OF FIGHTING. HIS CONSTANT COMPANION IS DOGMATIX, THE ONLY KNOWN CANINE ECOLOGIST, WHO HOWLS WITH DESPAIR WHEN A TREE IS CUT DOWN.

GETAFIX, THE VENERABLE VILLAGE DRUID, GATHERS MISTLETOE AND BREWS MAGIC POTIONS. HIS SPECIALITY IS THE POTION WHICH GIVES THE DRINKER SUPERHUMAN STRENGTH. BUT GETAFIX ALSO HAS OTHER RECIPES UP HIS SLEEVE . . .

CACOFONIX, THE BARD. OPINION IS DIVIDED AS TO HIS MUSICAL GIFTS. CACOFONIX THINKS HE'S A GENIUS. EVERY-ONE ELSE THINKS HE'S UNSPEAKABLE. BUT SO LONG AS HE DOESN'T SPEAK, LET ALONE SING, EVERYBODY LIKES HIM . . .

FINALLY, VITALSTATISTIX, THE CHIEF OF THE TRIBE. MAJESTIC, BRAVE AND HOT-TEMPERED, THE OLD WARRIOR IS RESPECTED BY HIS MEN AND FEARED BY HIS ENEMIES. VITALSTATISTIX HIMSELF HAS ONLY ONE FEAR, HE IS AFRAID THE SKY MAY FALL ON HIS HEAD TOMORROW. BUT AS HE ALWAYS SAYS, TOMORROW NEVER COMES.

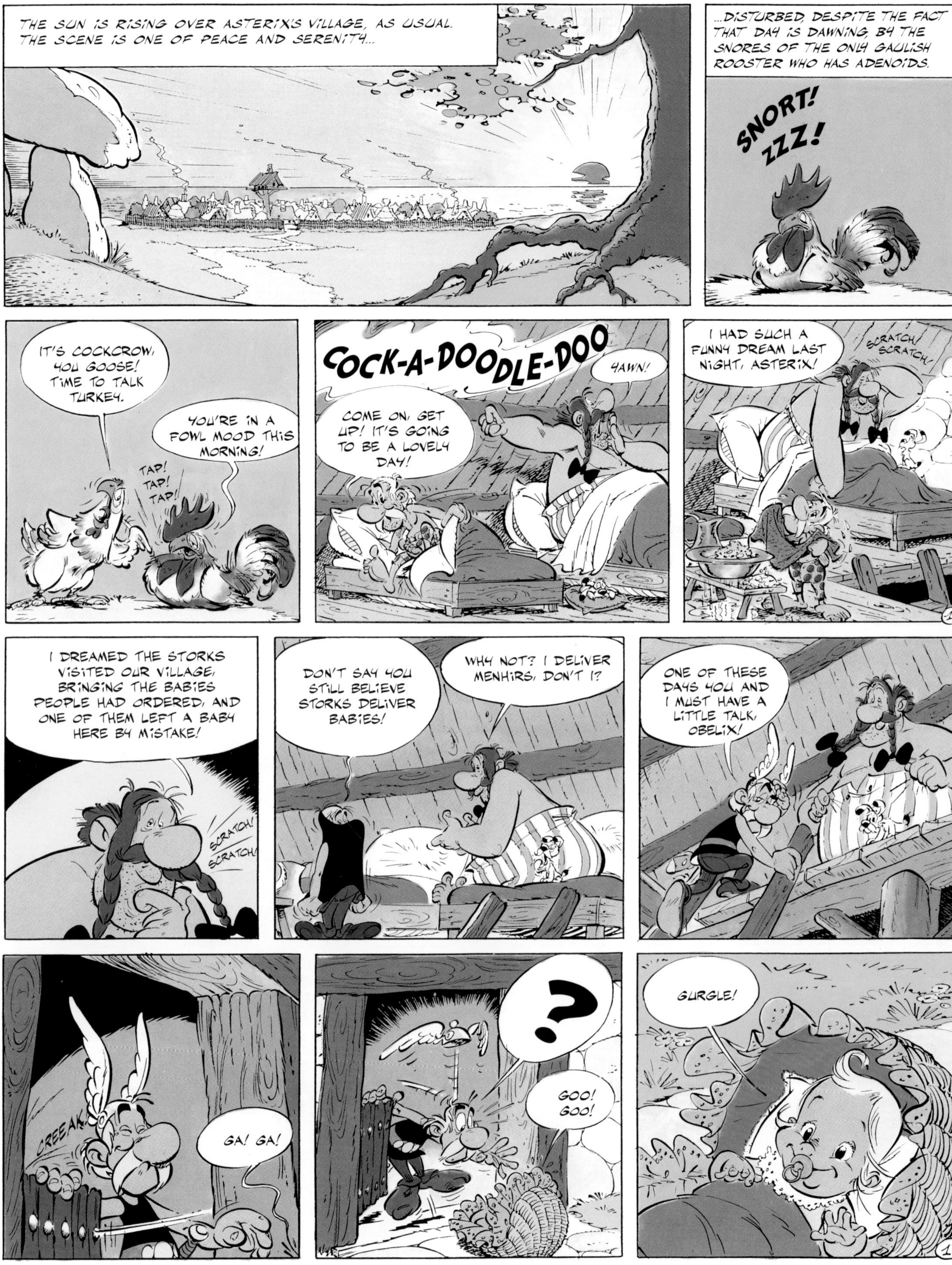
THE SUN IS RISING OVER ASTERIX'S VILLAGE, AS USUAL. THE SCENE IS ONE OF PEACE AND SERENITY...
...DISTURBED, DESPITE THE FACT THAT DAY IS DAWNING, BY THE SNORES OF THE ONLY GAULISH ROOSTER WHO HAS ADENOIDS.
SNORT! ZZZ!
IT'S COCKCROW, YOU GOOSE! TIME TO TALK TURKEY.
TAP! TAP! TAP!
YOU'RE IN A FOWL MOOD THIS MORNING!
COCK-A-DOODLE-DOO
YAWN!
COME ON, GET UP! IT'S GOING TO BE A LOVELY DAY!
I HAD SUCH A FUNNY DREAM LAST NIGHT, ASTERIX!
SCRATCH! SCRATCH!
I DREAMED THE STORKS VISITED OUR VILLAGE, BRINGING THE BABIES PEOPLE HAD ORDERED, AND ONE OF THEM LEFT A BABY HERE BY MISTAKE!
SCRATCH! SCRATCH!
DON'T SAY YOU STILL BELIEVE STORKS DELIVER BABIES!
WHY NOT? I DELIVER MENHIRS, DON'T I?
ONE OF THESE DAYS YOU AND I MUST HAVE A LITTLE TALK, OBELIX!
CREEAK
GA! GA!
?
GOO! GOO!
GURGLE!

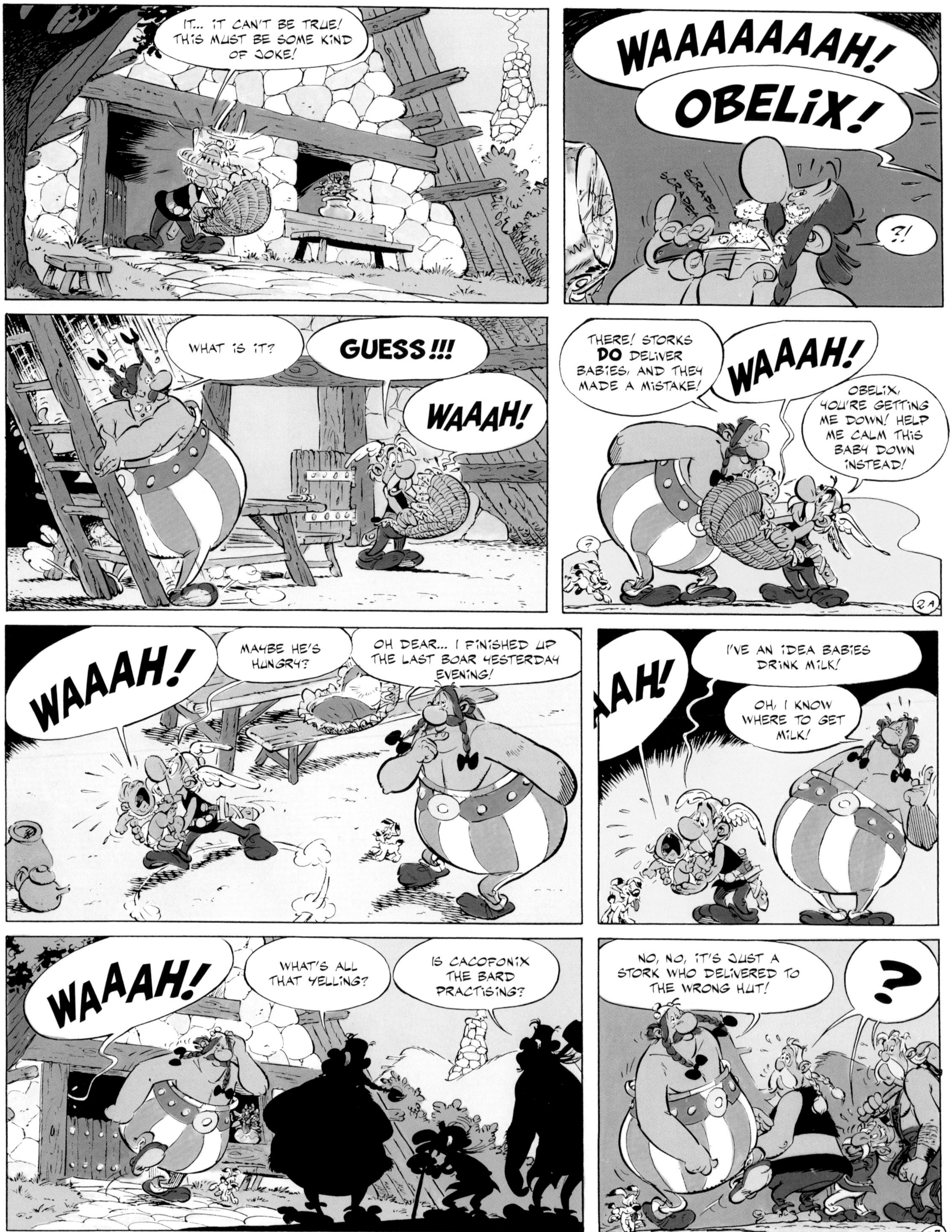

IT... IT CAN'T BE TRUE! THIS MUST BE SOME KIND OF JOKE!
WAAAAAAAH!
OBELIX!
SCRAPE! SCRAPE!
?!
WHAT IS IT?
GUESS!!!
WAAAH!
THERE! STORKS DO DELIVER BABIES, AND THEY MADE A MISTAKE!
WAAAH!
OBELIX, YOU'RE GETTING ME DOWN! HELP ME CALM THIS BABY DOWN INSTEAD!
?
WAAAH!
MAYBE HE'S HUNGRY?
OH DEAR... I FINISHED UP THE LAST BOAR YESTERDAY EVENING!
AAH!
I'VE AN IDEA BABIES DRINK MILK!
OH, I KNOW WHERE TO GET MILK!
WAAAH!
WHAT'S ALL THAT YELLING?
IS CACOFONIX THE BARD PRACTISING?
NO, NO, IT'S JUST A STORK WHO DELIVERED TO THE WRONG HUT!
?

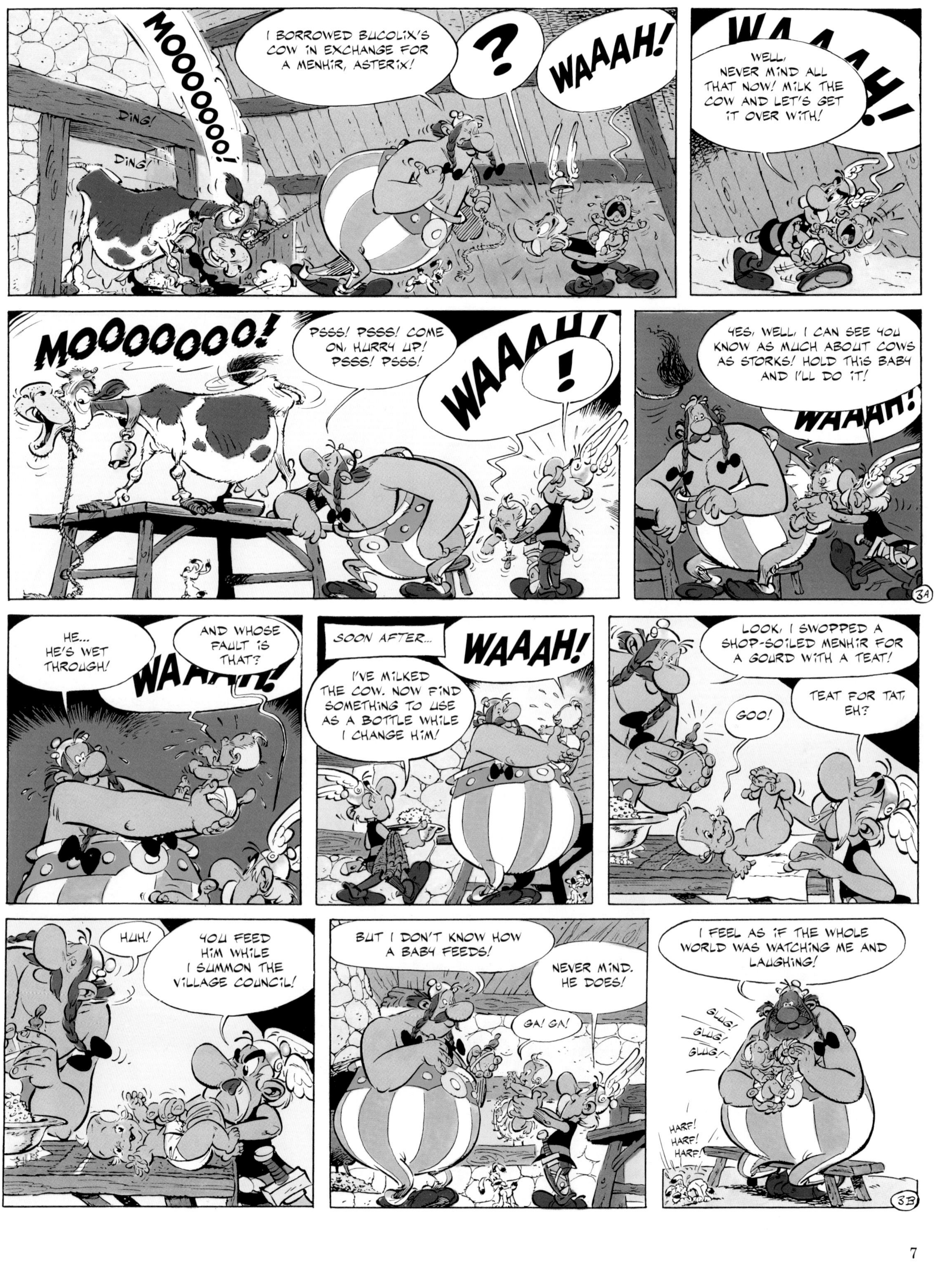
MOOOOOOO!
DING!
DING!
I BORROWED BUCOLIX'S COW IN EXCHANGE FOR A MENHIR, ASTERIX!
?
WAAAH!
WAAAAH!
WELL, NEVER MIND ALL THAT NOW! MILK THE COW AND LET'S GET IT OVER WITH!
MOOOOOOO!
PSSS! PSSS! COME ON, HURRY UP! PSSS! PSSS!
WAAAH!
!
YES, WELL, I CAN SEE YOU KNOW AS MUCH ABOUT COWS AS STORKS! HOLD THIS BABY AND I'LL DO IT!
WAAAH!
3A
HE... HE'S WET THROUGH!
AND WHOSE FAULT IS THAT?
WAAAH!
SOON AFTER...
WAAAH!
I'VE MILKED THE COW. NOW FIND SOMETHING TO USE AS A BOTTLE WHILE I CHANGE HIM!
LOOK, I SWOPPED A SHOP-SOILED MENHIR FOR A GOURD WITH A TEAT!
GOO!
TEAT FOR TAT, EH?
HUH!
YOU FEED HIM WHILE I SUMMON THE VILLAGE COUNCIL!
BUT I DON'T KNOW HOW A BABY FEEDS!
NEVER MIND. HE DOES!
GA! GA!
I FEEL AS IF THE WHOLE WORLD WAS WATCHING ME AND LAUGHING!
GLUG!
GLUG!
GLUG!
HARF!
HARF!
HARF!
3B

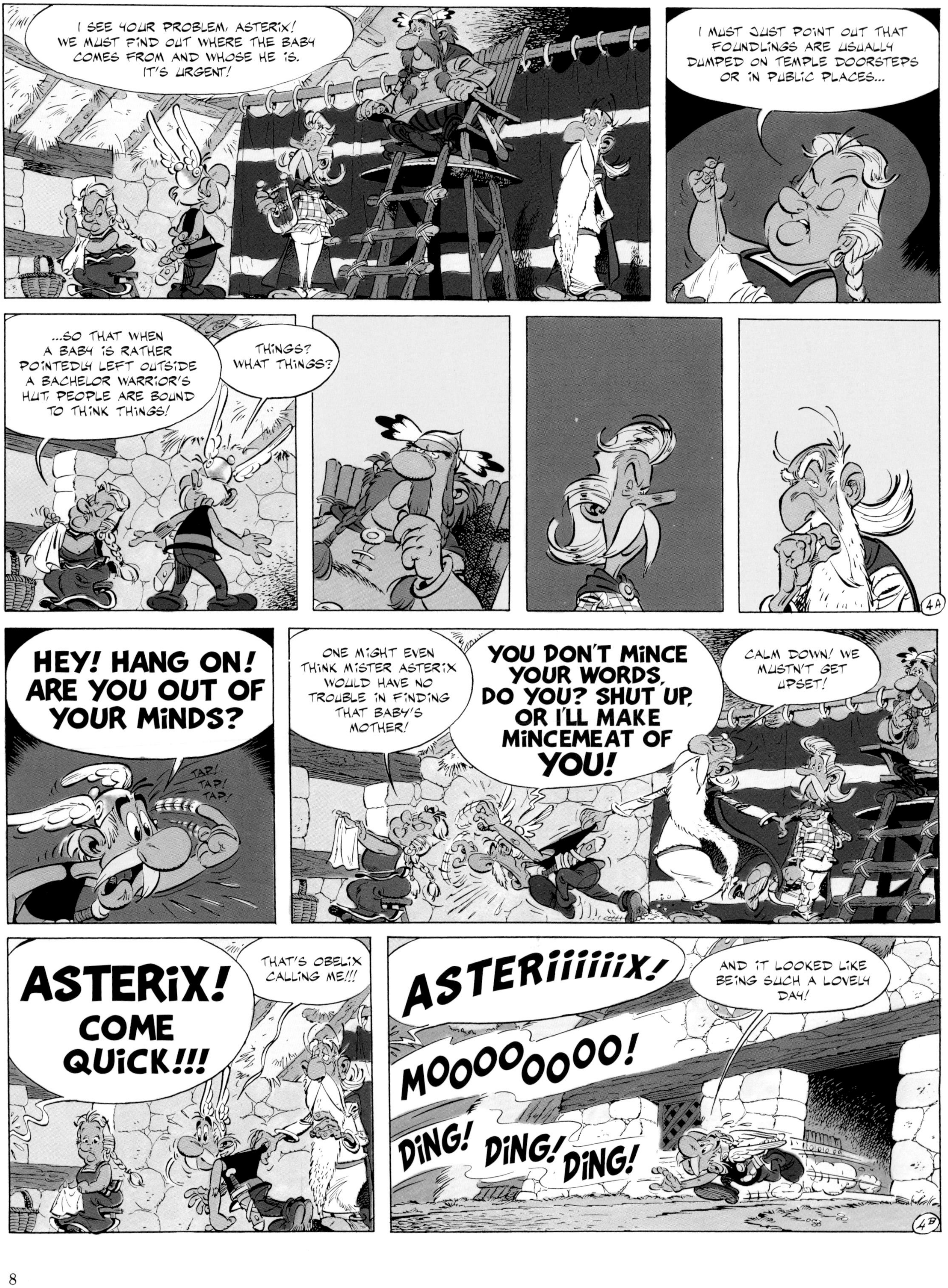

I SEE YOUR PROBLEM, ASTERIX! WE MUST FIND OUT WHERE THE BABY COMES FROM AND WHOSE HE IS. IT'S URGENT!
I MUST JUST POINT OUT THAT FOUNDLINGS ARE USUALLY DUMPED ON TEMPLE DOORSTEPS OR IN PUBLIC PLACES...
...SO THAT WHEN A BABY IS RATHER POINTEDLY LEFT OUTSIDE A BACHELOR WARRIOR'S HUT, PEOPLE ARE BOUND TO THINK THINGS!
THINGS? WHAT THINGS?
4A
HEY! HANG ON! ARE YOU OUT OF YOUR MINDS?
TAP! TAP! TAP!
ONE MIGHT EVEN THINK MISTER ASTERIX WOULD HAVE NO TROUBLE IN FINDING THAT BABY'S MOTHER!
YOU DON'T MINCE YOUR WORDS, DO YOU? SHUT UP, OR I'LL MAKE MINCEMEAT OF YOU!
CALM DOWN! WE MUSTN'T GET UPSET!
ASTERIX! COME QUICK!!!
THAT'S OBELIX CALLING ME!!!
ASTERIIIIIIX!
AND IT LOOKED LIKE BEING SUCH A LOVELY DAY!
MOOOOOOOO!
DING! DING! DING!
4B

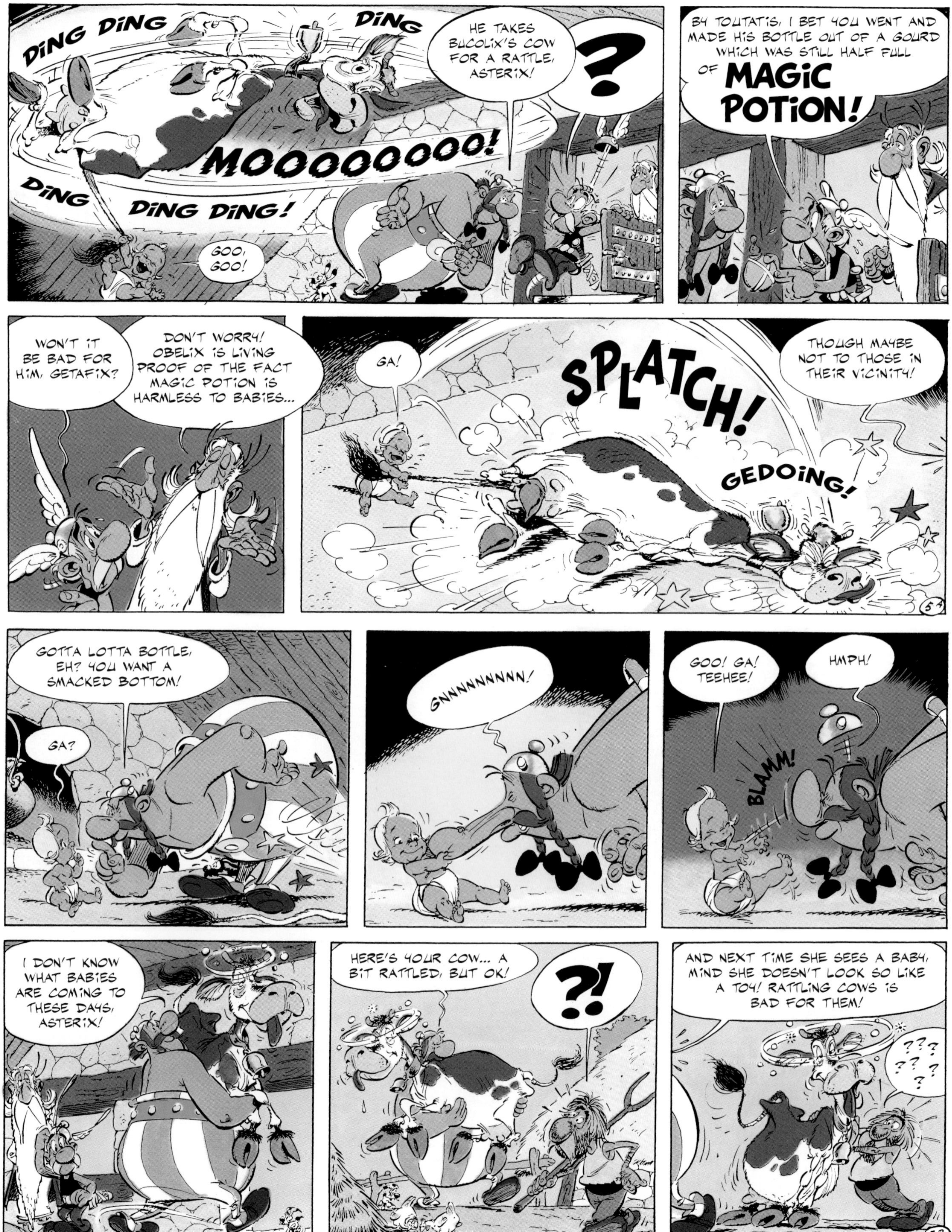

DING DING
DING
I
MOOOOOOOO!
DING
DING DING!
GOO, GOO!
HE TAKES BUCOLIX'S COW FOR A RATTLE, ASTERIX!
?
BY TOUTATIS, I BET YOU WENT AND MADE HIS BOTTLE OUT OF A GOURD WHICH WAS STILL HALF FULL OF MAGIC POTION!
WON'T IT BE BAD FOR HIM, GETAFIX?
DON'T WORRY! OBELIX IS LIVING PROOF OF THE FACT MAGIC POTION IS HARMLESS TO BABIES...
GA!
SPLATCH!
THOUGH MAYBE NOT TO THOSE IN THEIR VICINITY!
GEDOING!
GOTTA LOTTA BOTTLE, EH? YOU WANT A SMACKED BOTTOM!
GA?
GNNNNNNNN!
GOO! GA! TEEHEE!
HMPH!
BLAMM!
I DON'T KNOW WHAT BABIES ARE COMING TO THESE DAYS, ASTERIX!
HERE'S YOUR COW... A BIT RATTLED, BUT OK!
?!
AND NEXT TIME SHE SEES A BABY, MIND SHE DOESN'T LOOK SO LIKE A TOY! RATTLING COWS IS BAD FOR THEM!
???
??
?

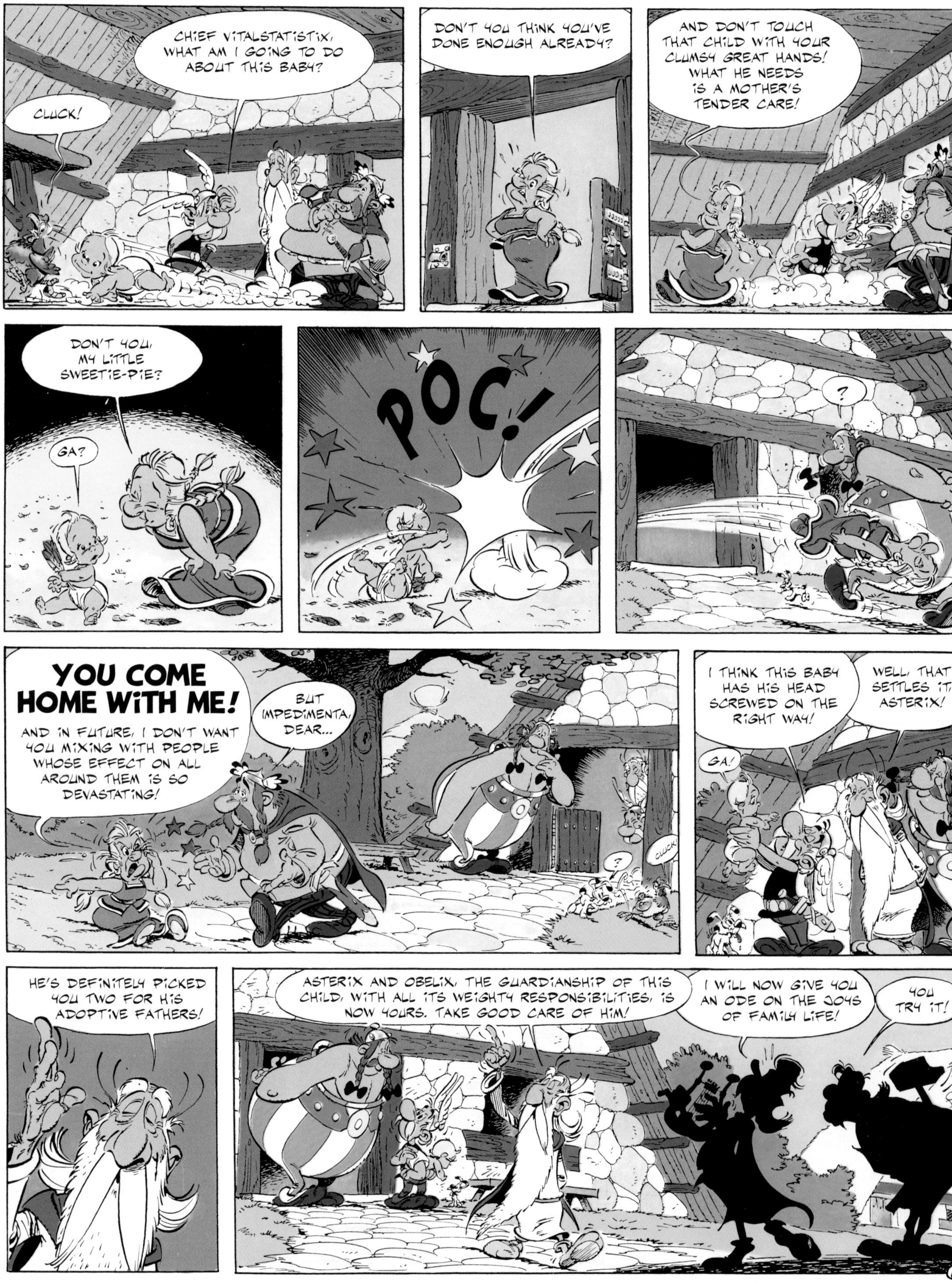

CHIEF VITALSTATISTIX, WHAT AM I GOING TO DO ABOUT THIS BABY?
CLUCK!
DON'T YOU THINK YOU'VE DONE ENOUGH ALREADY?
AND DON'T TOUCH THAT CHILD WITH YOUR CLUMSY GREAT HANDS! WHAT HE NEEDS IS A MOTHER'S TENDER CARE!
DON'T YOU, MY LITTLE SWEETIE-PIE?
GA?
POC!
?
YOU COME HOME WITH ME!
AND IN FUTURE, I DON'T WANT YOU MIXING WITH PEOPLE WHOSE EFFECT ON ALL AROUND THEM IS SO DEVASTATING!
BUT IMPEDIMENTA, DEAR...
?
CLUCK!
I THINK THIS BABY HAS HIS HEAD SCREWED ON THE RIGHT WAY!
WELL, THAT SETTLES IT, ASTERIX!
GA!
HE'S DEFINITELY PICKED YOU TWO FOR HIS ADOPTIVE FATHERS!
ASTERIX AND OBELIX, THE GUARDIANSHIP OF THIS CHILD, WITH ALL ITS WEIGHTY RESPONSIBILITIES, IS NOW YOURS. TAKE GOOD CARE OF HIM!
I WILL NOW GIVE YOU AN ODE ON THE JOYS OF FAMILY LIFE!
YOU TRY IT!

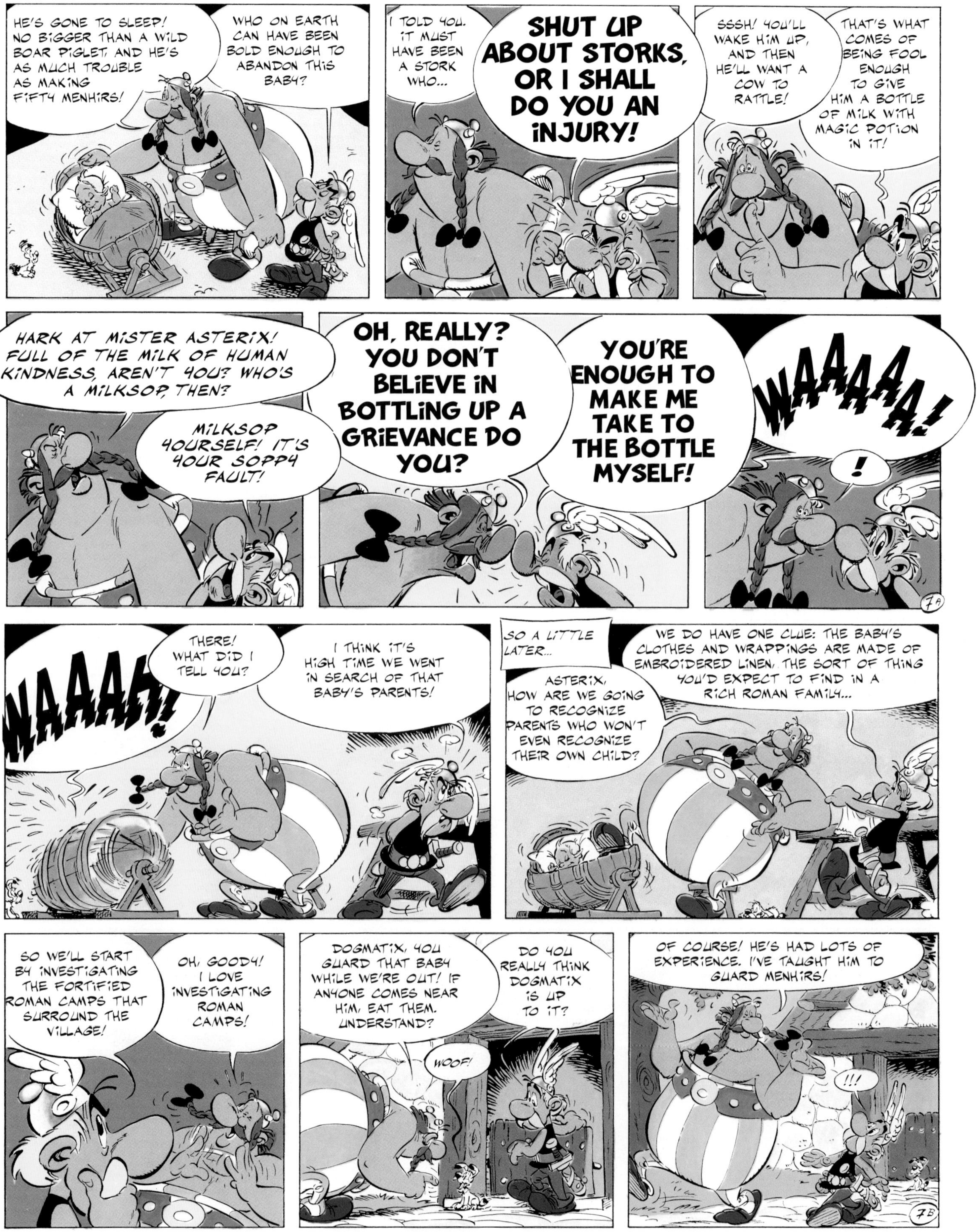

HE'S GONE TO SLEEP! NO BIGGER THAN A WILD BOAR PIGLET, AND HE'S AS MUCH TROUBLE AS MAKING FIFTY MENHIRS!
WHO ON EARTH CAN HAVE BEEN BOLD ENOUGH TO ABANDON THIS BABY?
I TOLD YOU. IT MUST HAVE BEEN A STORK WHO...
SHUT UP ABOUT STORKS, OR I SHALL DO YOU AN INJURY!
SSSH! YOU'LL WAKE HIM UP, AND THEN HE'LL WANT A COW TO RATTLE!
THAT'S WHAT COMES OF BEING FOOL ENOUGH TO GIVE HIM A BOTTLE OF MILK WITH MAGIC POTION IN IT!
HARK AT MISTER ASTERIX! FULL OF THE MILK OF HUMAN KINDNESS, AREN'T YOU? WHO'S A MILKSOP, THEN?
MILKSOP YOURSELF! IT'S YOUR SOPPY FAULT!
OH, REALLY? YOU DON'T BELIEVE IN BOTTLING UP A GRIEVANCE DO YOU?
YOU'RE ENOUGH TO MAKE ME TAKE TO THE BOTTLE MYSELF!
WAAAAA!
!
WAAAH!
THERE! WHAT DID I TELL YOU?
I THINK IT'S HIGH TIME WE WENT IN SEARCH OF THAT BABY'S PARENTS!
SO A LITTLE LATER...
ASTERIX, HOW ARE WE GOING TO RECOGNIZE PARENTS WHO WON'T EVEN RECOGNIZE THEIR OWN CHILD?
WE DO HAVE ONE CLUE: THE BABY'S CLOTHES AND WRAPPINGS ARE MADE OF EMBROIDERED LINEN, THE SORT OF THING YOU'D EXPECT TO FIND IN A RICH ROMAN FAMILY...
SO WE'LL START BY INVESTIGATING THE FORTIFIED ROMAN CAMPS THAT SURROUND THE VILLAGE!
OH, GOODY! I LOVE INVESTIGATING ROMAN CAMPS!
DOGMATIX, YOU GUARD THAT BABY WHILE WE'RE OUT! IF ANYONE COMES NEAR HIM, EAT THEM. UNDERSTAND?
DO YOU REALLY THINK DOGMATIX IS UP TO IT?
WOOF!
OF COURSE! HE'S HAD LOTS OF EXPERIENCE. I'VE TAUGHT HIM TO GUARD MENHIRS!
!!!

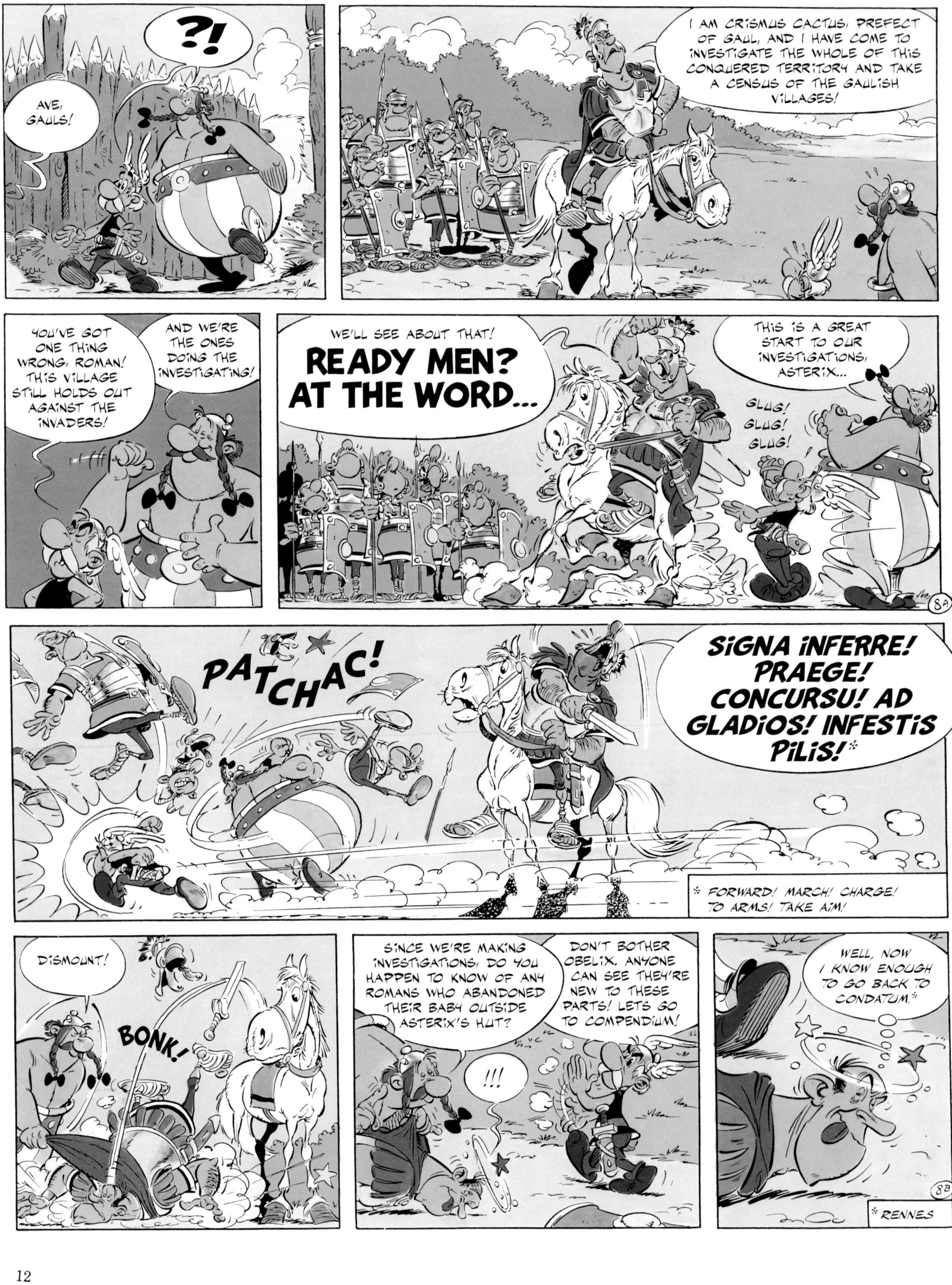
AVE, GAULS!
?!
I AM CRISMUS CACTUS, PREFECT OF GAUL, AND I HAVE COME TO INVESTIGATE THE WHOLE OF THIS CONQUERED TERRITORY AND TAKE A CENSUS OF THE GAULISH VILLAGES!
YOU'VE GOT ONE THING WRONG, ROMAN! THIS VILLAGE STILL HOLDS OUT AGAINST THE INVADERS!
AND WE'RE THE ONES DOING THE INVESTIGATING!
WE'LL SEE ABOUT THAT!
READY MEN? AT THE WORD...
THIS IS A GREAT START TO OUR INVESTIGATIONS, ASTERIX...
GLUG! GLUG! GLUG!
8A
PATCHAC!
SIGNA INFERRE! PRAEGE! CONCURSU! AD GLADIOS! INFESTIS PILIS!*
* FORWARD! MARCH! CHARGE! TO ARMS! TAKE AIM!
DISMOUNT!
BONK!
SINCE WE'RE MAKING INVESTIGATIONS, DO YOU HAPPEN TO KNOW OF ANY ROMANS WHO ABANDONED THEIR BABY OUTSIDE ASTERIX'S HUT?
DON'T BOTHER OBELIX. ANYONE CAN SEE THEY'RE NEW TO THESE PARTS! LETS GO TO COMPENDIUM!
!!!
WELL, NOW I KNOW ENOUGH TO GO BACK TO CONDATUM.*
8B
* RENNES

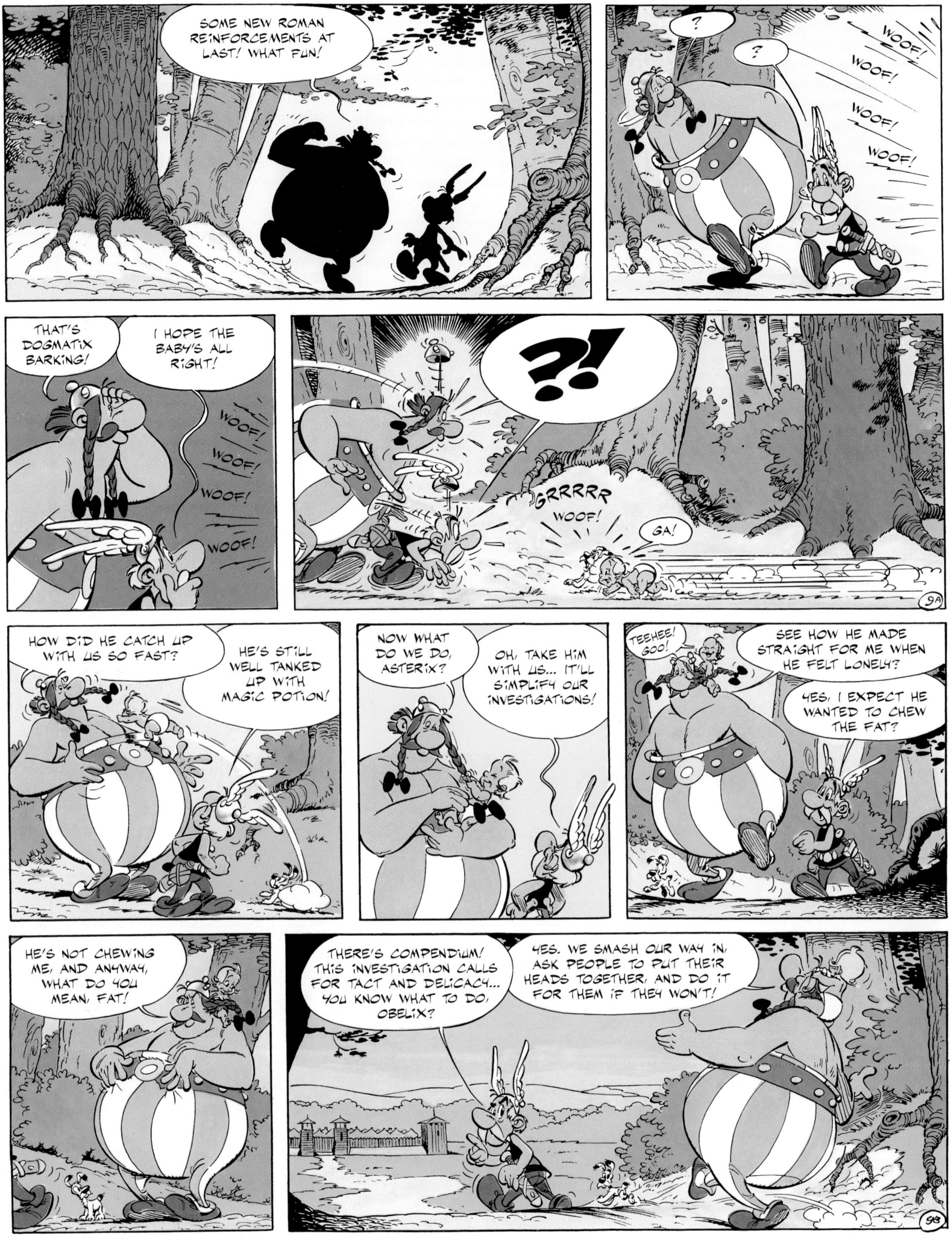
SOME NEW ROMAN REINFORCEMENTS AT LAST! WHAT FUN!
?
?
WOOF!
WOOF!
WOOF!
WOOF!
THAT'S DOGMATIX BARKING!
I HOPE THE BABY'S ALL RIGHT!
WOOF!
WOOF!
WOOF!
WOOF!
?!
GRRRRR
WOOF!
GA!
HOW DID HE CATCH UP WITH US SO FAST?
HE'S STILL WELL TANKED UP WITH MAGIC POTION!
NOW WHAT DO WE DO, ASTERIX?
OH, TAKE HIM WITH US... IT'LL SIMPLIFY OUR INVESTIGATIONS!
TEEHEE! GOO!
SEE HOW HE MADE STRAIGHT FOR ME WHEN HE FELT LONELY?
YES, I EXPECT HE WANTED TO CHEW THE FAT?
HE'S NOT CHEWING ME, AND ANYWAY, WHAT DO YOU MEAN, FAT!
THERE'S COMPENDIUM! THIS INVESTIGATION CALLS FOR TACT AND DELICACY... YOU KNOW WHAT TO DO, OBELIX?
YES. WE SMASH OUR WAY IN, ASK PEOPLE TO PUT THEIR HEADS TOGETHER, AND DO IT FOR THEM IF THEY WON'T!

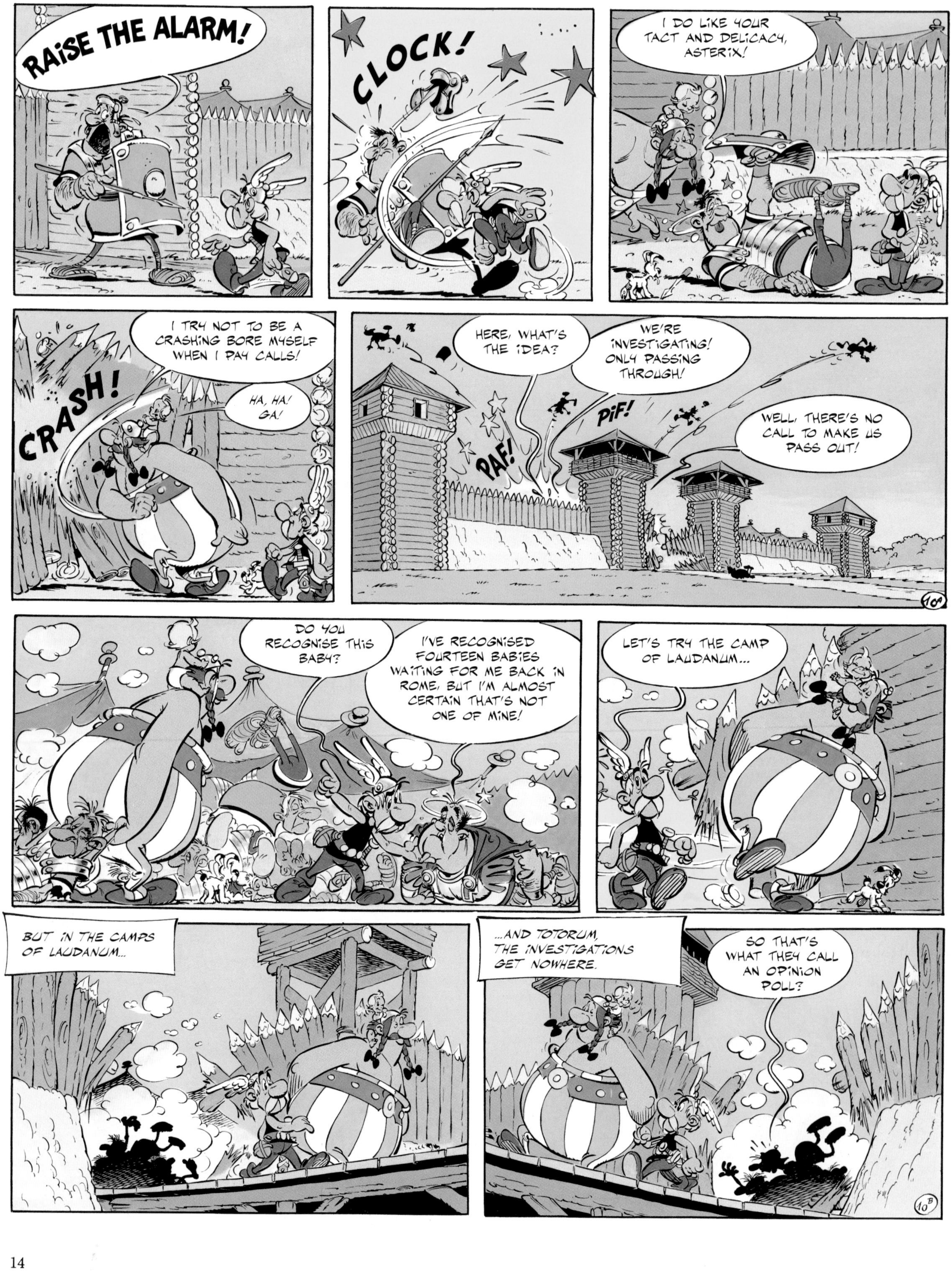
RAISE THE ALARM!
CLOCK!
I DO LIKE YOUR TACT AND DELICACY, ASTERIX!
CRASH!
I TRY NOT TO BE A CRASHING BORE MYSELF WHEN I PAY CALLS!
HA, HA! GA!
HERE, WHAT'S THE IDEA?
WE'RE INVESTIGATING! ONLY PASSING THROUGH!
PAF!
PIF!
WELL, THERE'S NO CALL TO MAKE US PASS OUT!
10A
DO YOU RECOGNISE THIS BABY?
I'VE RECOGNISED FOURTEEN BABIES WAITING FOR ME BACK IN ROME, BUT I'M ALMOST CERTAIN THAT'S NOT ONE OF MINE!
LET'S TRY THE CAMP OF LAUDANUM...
BUT IN THE CAMPS OF LAUDANUM...
...AND TOTORUM, THE INVESTIGATIONS GET NOWHERE.
SO THAT'S WHAT THEY CALL AN OPINION POLL?
10B

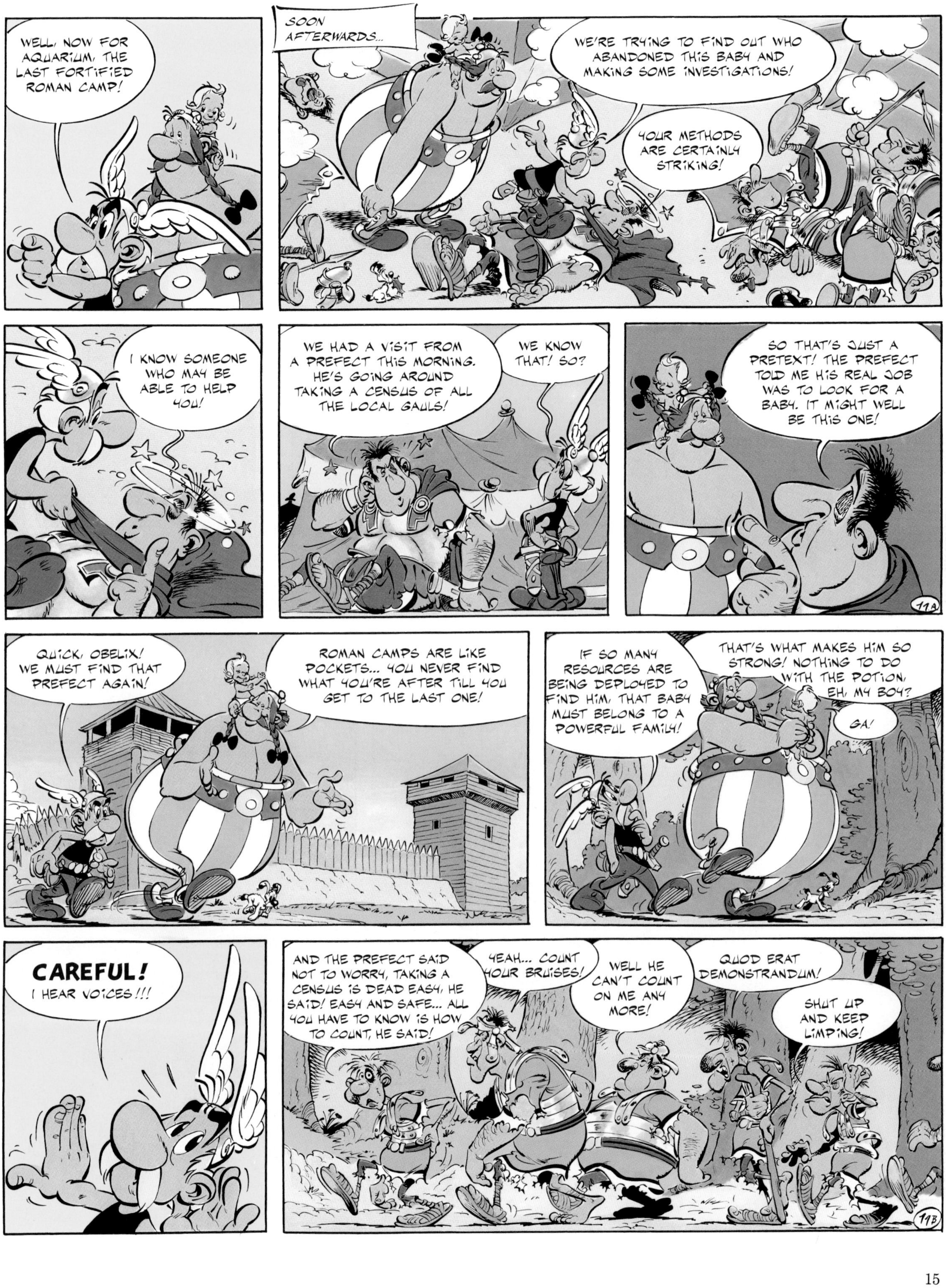
WELL, NOW FOR AQUARIUM, THE LAST FORTIFIED ROMAN CAMP!
SOON AFTERWARDS...
WE'RE TRYING TO FIND OUT WHO ABANDONED THIS BABY AND MAKING SOME INVESTIGATIONS!
YOUR METHODS ARE CERTAINLY STRIKING!
I KNOW SOMEONE WHO MAY BE ABLE TO HELP YOU!
WE HAD A VISIT FROM A PREFECT THIS MORNING. HE'S GOING AROUND TAKING A CENSUS OF ALL THE LOCAL GAULS!
WE KNOW THAT! SO?
SO THAT'S JUST A PRETEXT! THE PREFECT TOLD ME HIS REAL JOB WAS TO LOOK FOR A BABY. IT MIGHT WELL BE THIS ONE!
QUICK, OBELIX! WE MUST FIND THAT PREFECT AGAIN!
ROMAN CAMPS ARE LIKE POCKETS... YOU NEVER FIND WHAT YOU'RE AFTER TILL YOU GET TO THE LAST ONE!
IF SO MANY RESOURCES ARE BEING DEPLOYED TO FIND HIM, THAT BABY MUST BELONG TO A POWERFUL FAMILY!
THAT'S WHAT MAKES HIM SO STRONG! NOTHING TO DO WITH THE POTION, EH, MY BOY?
GA!
CAREFUL! I HEAR VOICES!!!
AND THE PREFECT SAID NOT TO WORRY, TAKING A CENSUS IS DEAD EASY, HE SAID! EASY AND SAFE... ALL YOU HAVE TO KNOW IS HOW TO COUNT, HE SAID!
YEAH... COUNT YOUR BRUISES!
WELL HE CAN'T COUNT ON ME ANY MORE!
QUOD ERAT DEMONSTRANDUM!
SHUT UP AND KEEP LIMPING!

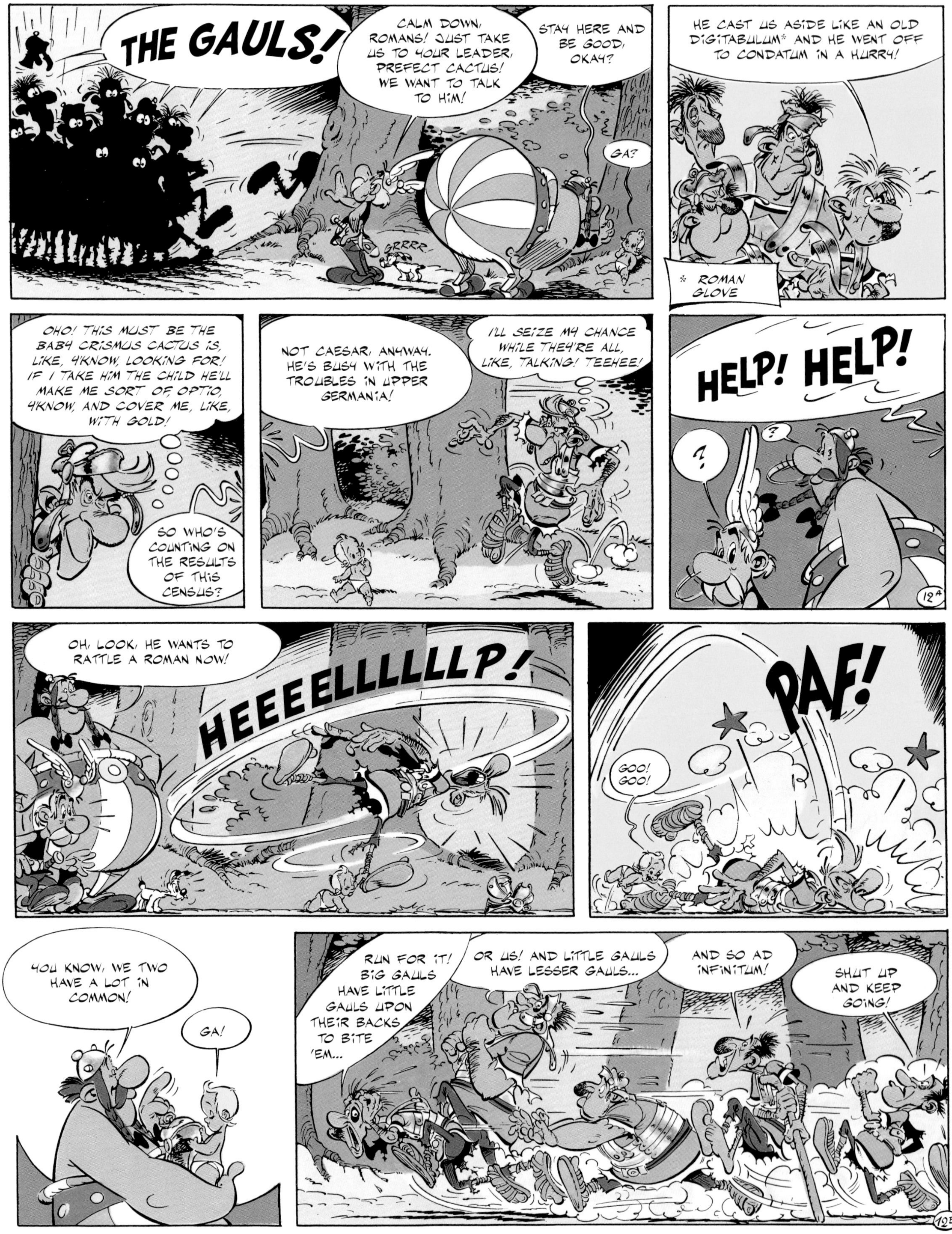
THE GAULS!
CALM DOWN, ROMANS! JUST TAKE US TO YOUR LEADER, PREFECT CACTUS! WE WANT TO TALK TO HIM!
STAY HERE AND BE GOOD, OKAY?
GA?
GRRRR!
HE CAST US ASIDE LIKE AN OLD DIGITABULUM* AND HE WENT OFF TO CONDATUM IN A HURRY!
* ROMAN GLOVE
OHO! THIS MUST BE THE BABY CRISMUS CACTUS IS, LIKE, Y'KNOW, LOOKING FOR! IF I TAKE HIM THE CHILD HE'LL MAKE ME SORT OF, OPTIO, Y'KNOW, AND COVER ME, LIKE, WITH GOLD!
SO WHO'S COUNTING ON THE RESULTS OF THIS CENSUS?
NOT CAESAR, ANYWAY. HE'S BUSY WITH THE TROUBLES IN UPPER GERMANIA!
I'LL SEIZE MY CHANCE WHILE THEY'RE ALL, LIKE, TALKING! TEEHEE!
HELP! HELP!
?
?
12A
OH, LOOK, HE WANTS TO RATTLE A ROMAN NOW!
HEEEELLLLLLP!
PAF!
GOO! GOO!
YOU KNOW, WE TWO HAVE A LOT IN COMMON!
GA!
RUN FOR IT! BIG GAULS HAVE LITTLE GAULS UPON THEIR BACKS TO BITE 'EM...
OR US! AND LITTLE GAULS HAVE LESSER GAULS...
AND SO AD INFINITUM!
SHUT UP AND KEEP GOING!
12B

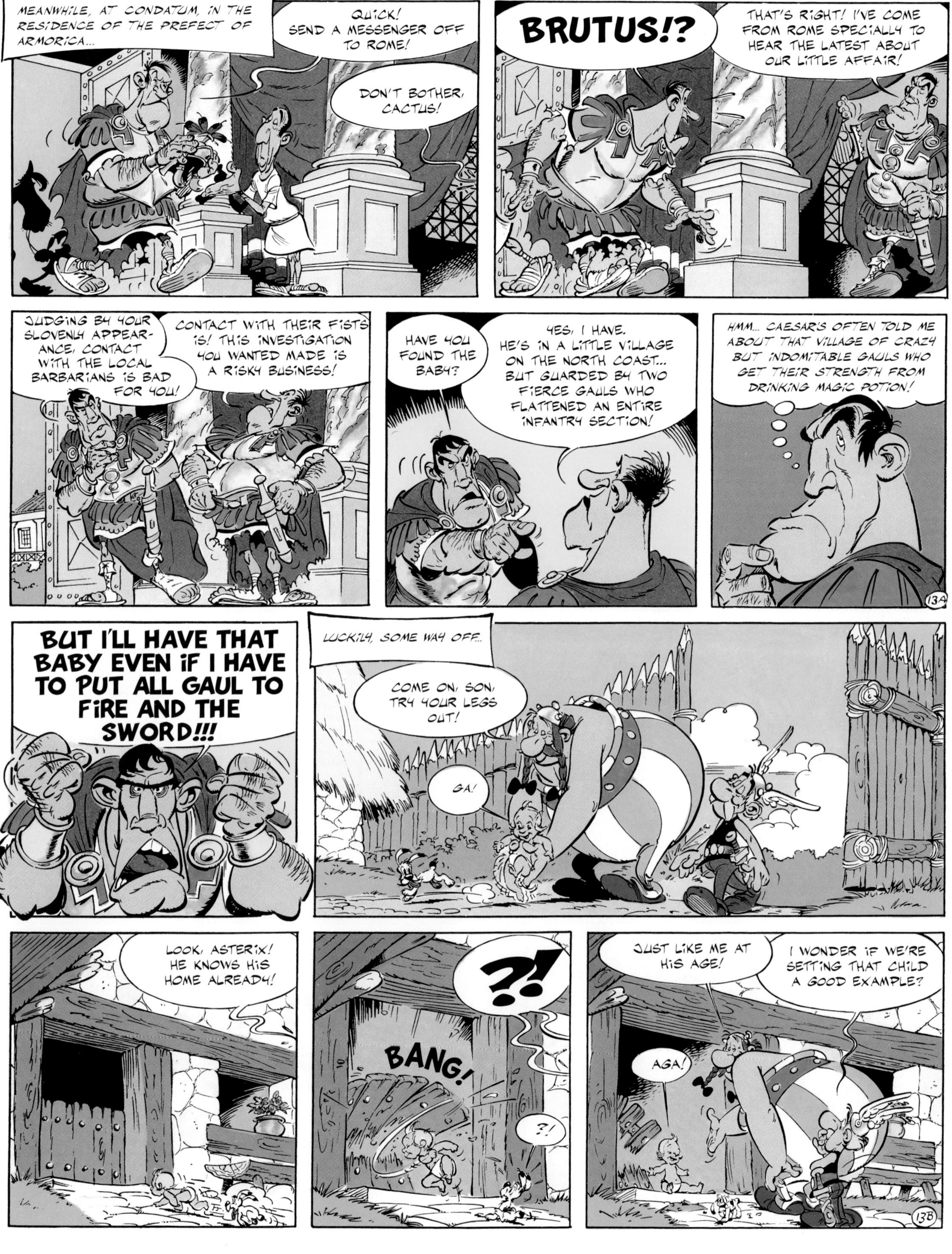
MEANWHILE, AT CONDATUM, IN THE RESIDENCE OF THE PREFECT OF ARMORICA...
QUICK! SEND A MESSENGER OFF TO ROME!
DON'T BOTHER, CACTUS!
BRUTUS!?
THAT'S RIGHT! I'VE COME FROM ROME SPECIALLY TO HEAR THE LATEST ABOUT OUR LITTLE AFFAIR!
JUDGING BY YOUR SLOVENLY APPEARANCE, CONTACT WITH THE LOCAL BARBARIANS IS BAD FOR YOU!
CONTACT WITH THEIR FISTS IS! THIS INVESTIGATION YOU WANTED MADE IS A RISKY BUSINESS!
HAVE YOU FOUND THE BABY?
YES, I HAVE. HE'S IN A LITTLE VILLAGE ON THE NORTH COAST... BUT GUARDED BY TWO FIERCE GAULS WHO FLATTENED AN ENTIRE INFANTRY SECTION!
HMM... CAESAR'S OFTEN TOLD ME ABOUT THAT VILLAGE OF CRAZY BUT INDOMITABLE GAULS WHO GET THEIR STRENGTH FROM DRINKING MAGIC POTION!
13A
BUT I'LL HAVE THAT BABY EVEN IF I HAVE TO PUT ALL GAUL TO FIRE AND THE SWORD!!!
LUCKILY, SOME WAY OFF...
COME ON, SON, TRY YOUR LEGS OUT!
GA!
LOOK, ASTERIX! HE KNOWS HIS HOME ALREADY!
?!
BANG!
?!
JUST LIKE ME AT HIS AGE!
I WONDER IF WE'RE SETTING THAT CHILD A GOOD EXAMPLE?
AGA!
13B

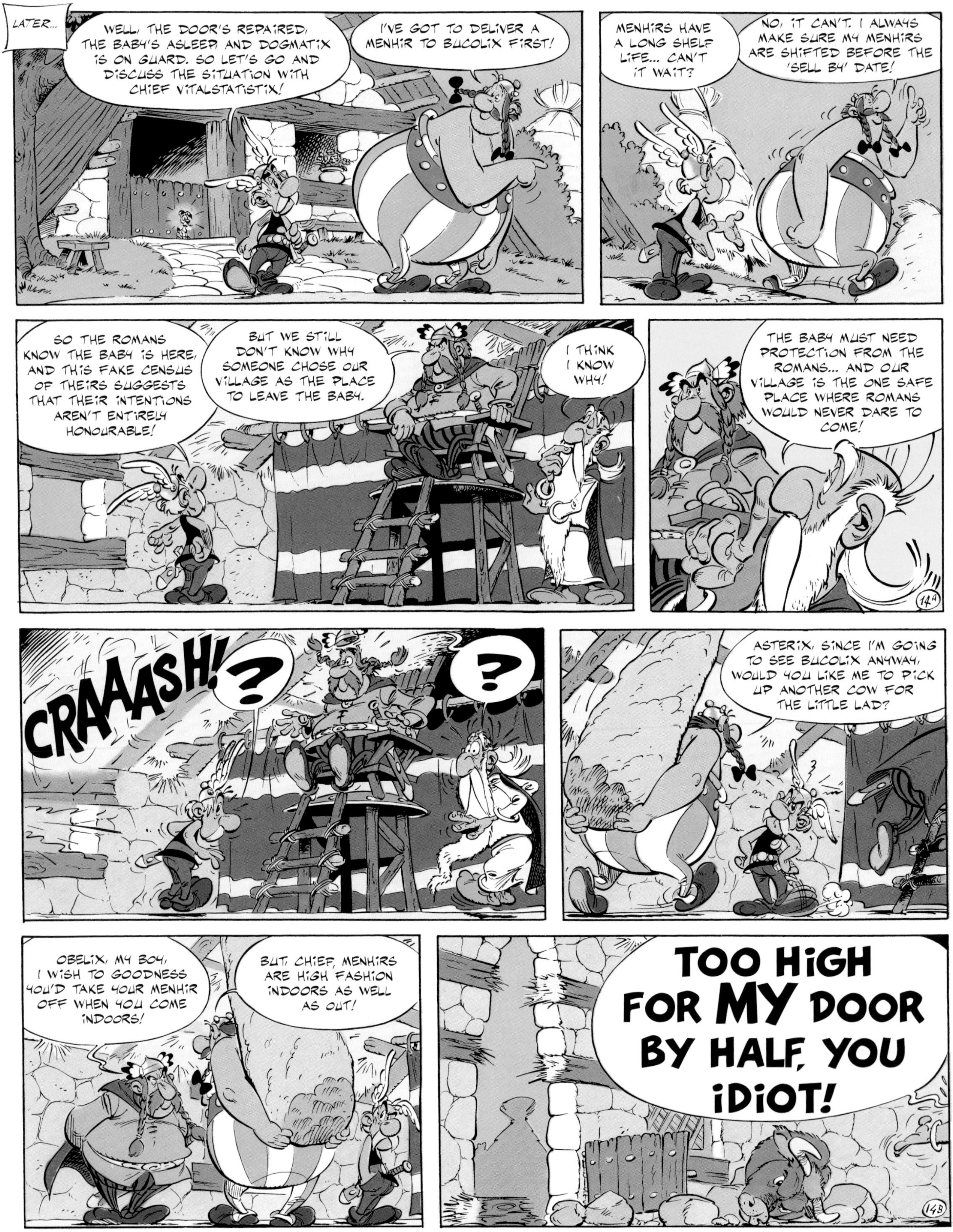
LATER...
WELL, THE DOOR'S REPAIRED, THE BABY'S ASLEEP, AND DOGMATIX IS ON GUARD. SO LET'S GO AND DISCUSS THE SITUATION WITH CHIEF VITALSTATISTIX!
I'VE GOT TO DELIVER A MENHIR TO BUCOLIX FIRST!
MENHIRS HAVE A LONG SHELF LIFE... CAN'T IT WAIT?
NO, IT CAN'T. I ALWAYS MAKE SURE MY MENHIRS ARE SHIFTED BEFORE THE 'SELL BY' DATE!
SO THE ROMANS KNOW THE BABY IS HERE, AND THIS FAKE CENSUS OF THEIRS SUGGESTS THAT THEIR INTENTIONS AREN'T ENTIRELY HONOURABLE!
BUT WE STILL DON'T KNOW WHY SOMEONE CHOSE OUR VILLAGE AS THE PLACE TO LEAVE THE BABY.
I THINK I KNOW WHY!
THE BABY MUST NEED PROTECTION FROM THE ROMANS... AND OUR VILLAGE IS THE ONE SAFE PLACE WHERE ROMANS WOULD NEVER DARE TO COME!
14A
CRAAASH!
?
?
ASTERIX, SINCE I'M GOING TO SEE BUCOLIX ANYWAY, WOULD YOU LIKE ME TO PICK UP ANOTHER COW FOR THE LITTLE LAD?
OBELIX, MY BOY, I WISH TO GOODNESS YOU'D TAKE YOUR MENHIR OFF WHEN YOU COME INDOORS!
BUT, CHIEF, MENHIRS ARE HIGH FASHION INDOORS AS WELL AS OUT!
TOO HIGH FOR MY DOOR BY HALF, YOU IDIOT!
14B

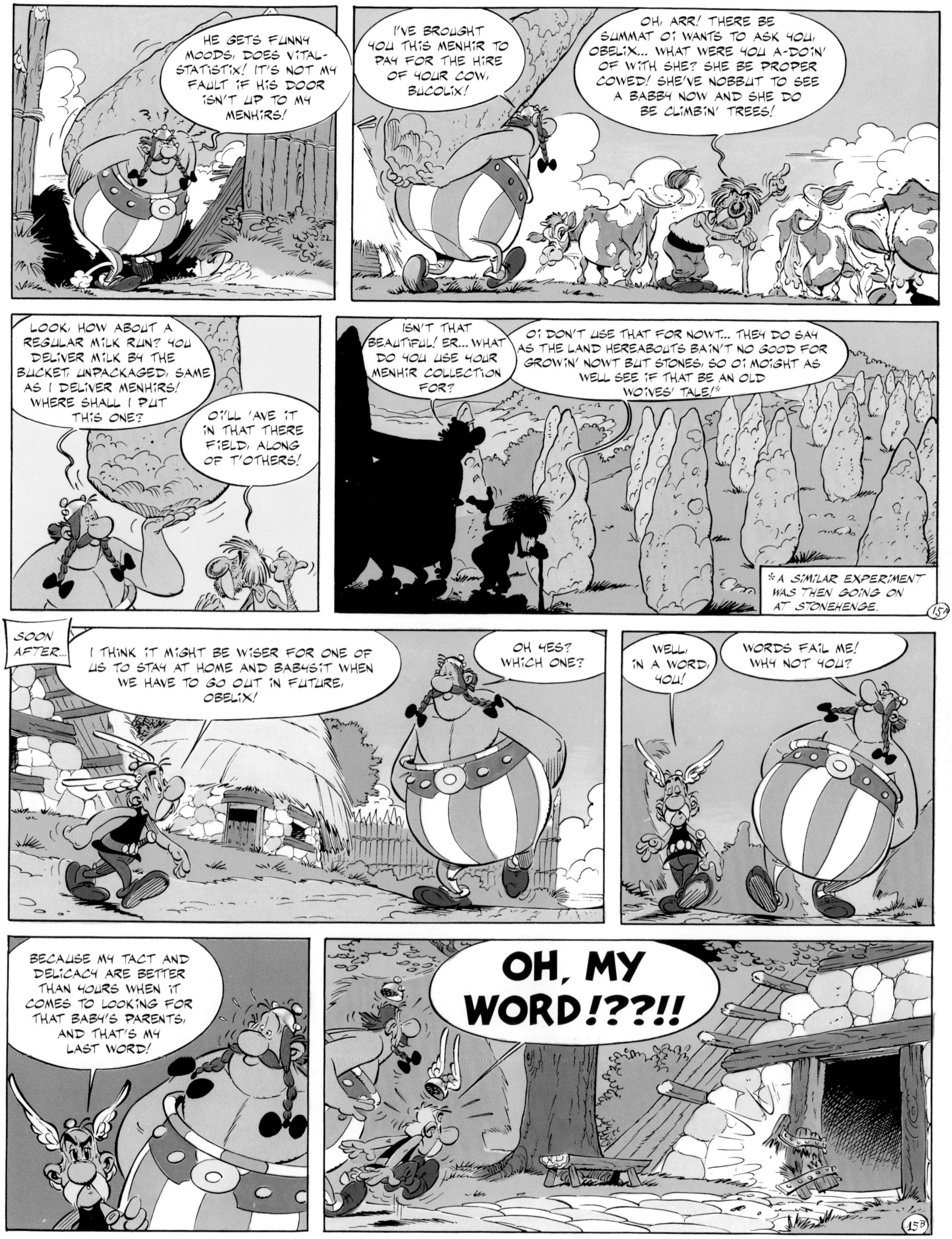
HE GETS FUNNY MOODS, DOES VITAL-STATISTIX! IT'S NOT MY FAULT IF HIS DOOR ISN'T UP TO MY MENHIRS!
I'VE BROUGHT YOU THIS MENHIR TO PAY FOR THE HIRE OF YOUR COW, BUCOLIX!
OH, ARR! THERE BE SUMMAT OI WANTS TO ASK YOU, OBELIX... WHAT WERE YOU A-DOIN' OF WITH SHE? SHE BE PROPER COWED! SHE'VE NOBBUT TO SEE A BABBY NOW AND SHE DO BE CLIMBIN' TREES!
LOOK, HOW ABOUT A REGULAR MILK RUN? YOU DELIVER MILK BY THE BUCKET, UNPACKAGED, SAME AS I DELIVER MENHIRS! WHERE SHALL I PUT THIS ONE?
OI'LL 'AVE IT IN THAT THERE FIELD, ALONG OF T'OTHERS!
ISN'T THAT BEAUTIFUL! ER... WHAT DO YOU USE YOUR MENHIR COLLECTION FOR?
OI DON'T USE THAT FOR NOWT... THEY DO SAY AS THE LAND HEREABOUTS BAIN'T NO GOOD FOR GROWIN' NOWT BUT STONES, SO OI MOIGHT AS WELL SEE IF THAT BE AN OLD WOIVES' TALE!*
* A SIMILAR EXPERIMENT WAS THEN GOING ON AT STONEHENGE.
15A
SOON AFTER...
I THINK IT MIGHT BE WISER FOR ONE OF US TO STAY AT HOME AND BABYSIT WHEN WE HAVE TO GO OUT IN FUTURE, OBELIX!
OH YES? WHICH ONE?
WELL, IN A WORD, YOU!
WORDS FAIL ME! WHY NOT YOU?
BECAUSE MY TACT AND DELICACY ARE BETTER THAN YOURS WHEN IT COMES TO LOOKING FOR THAT BABY'S PARENTS, AND THAT'S MY LAST WORD!
OH, MY WORD!??!!
15B

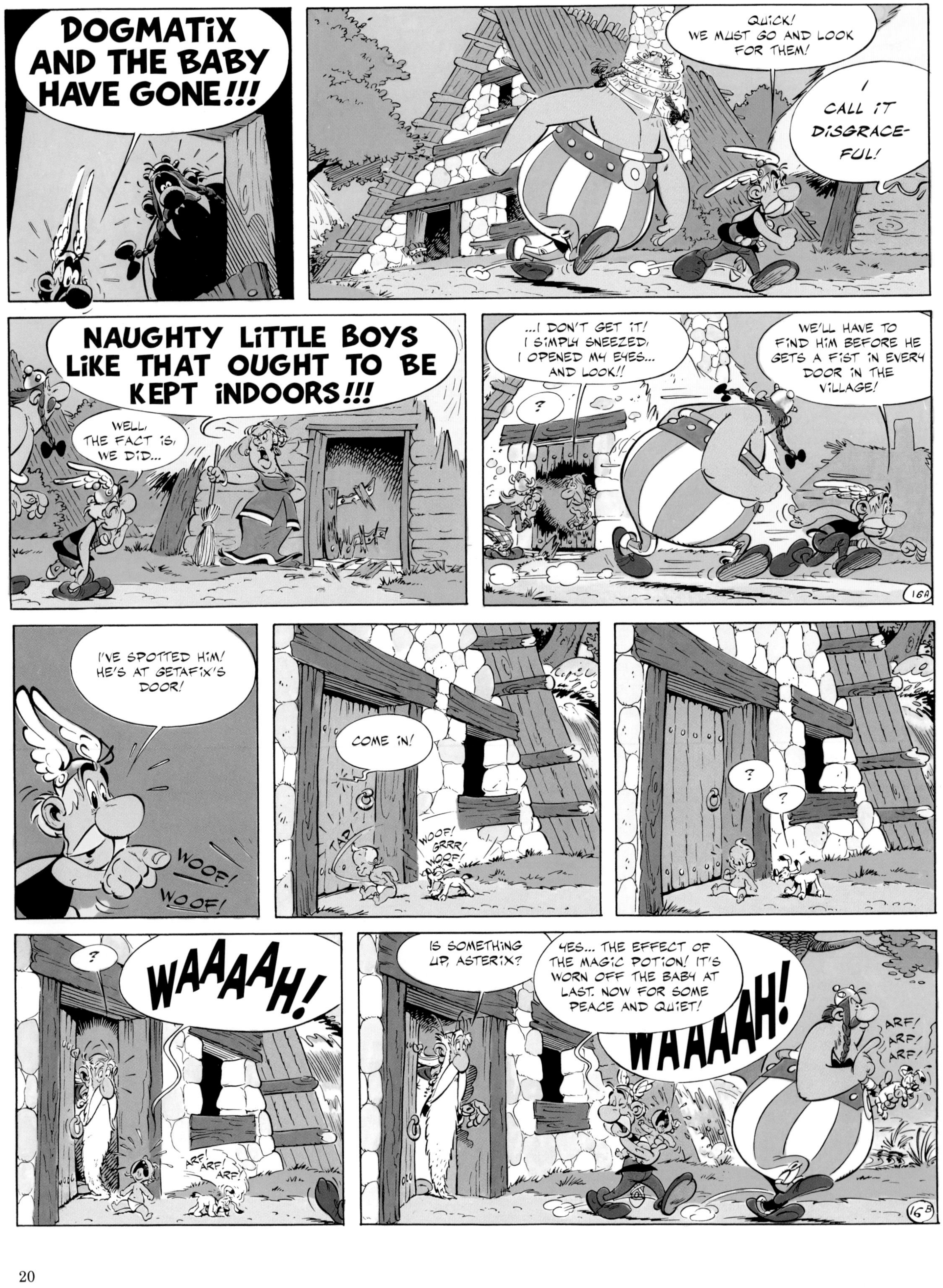
DOGMATIX AND THE BABY HAVE GONE!!!
QUICK! WE MUST GO AND LOOK FOR THEM!
I CALL IT DISGRACE-FUL!
NAUGHTY LITTLE BOYS LIKE THAT OUGHT TO BE KEPT INDOORS!!!
WELL, THE FACT IS, WE DID...
?
...I DON'T GET IT! I SIMPLY SNEEZED, I OPENED MY EYES... AND LOOK!!
WE'LL HAVE TO FIND HIM BEFORE HE GETS A FIST IN EVERY DOOR IN THE VILLAGE!
I'VE SPOTTED HIM! HE'S AT GETAFIX'S DOOR!
WOOF! WOOF!
COME IN!
TAP!
WOOF! GRRR! WOOF!
?
?
?
WAAAAH!
ARF! ARF! ARF!
IS SOMETHING UP, ASTERIX?
YES... THE EFFECT OF THE MAGIC POTION! IT'S WORN OFF THE BABY AT LAST. NOW FOR SOME PEACE AND QUIET!
WAAAAH!
ARF! ARF! ARF!

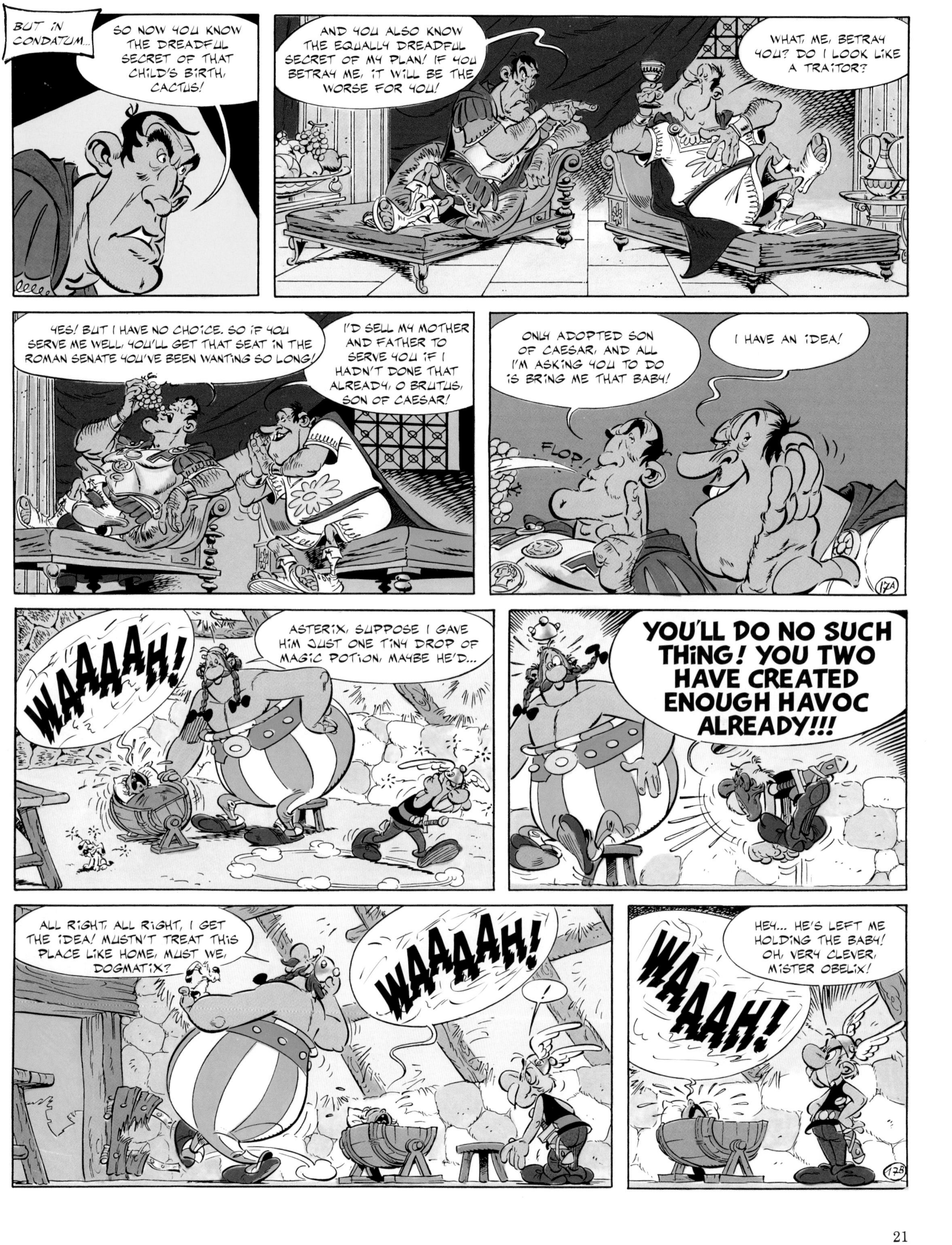

BUT IN CONDATUM...
SO NOW YOU KNOW THE DREADFUL SECRET OF THAT CHILD'S BIRTH, CACTUS!
AND YOU ALSO KNOW THE EQUALLY DREADFUL SECRET OF MY PLAN! IF YOU BETRAY ME, IT WILL BE THE WORSE FOR YOU!
WHAT, ME, BETRAY YOU? DO I LOOK LIKE A TRAITOR?
YES! BUT I HAVE NO CHOICE. SO IF YOU SERVE ME WELL, YOU'LL GET THAT SEAT IN THE ROMAN SENATE YOU'VE BEEN WANTING SO LONG!
I'D SELL MY MOTHER AND FATHER TO SERVE YOU IF I HADN'T DONE THAT ALREADY, O BRUTUS, SON OF CAESAR!
ONLY ADOPTED SON OF CAESAR, AND ALL I'M ASKING YOU TO DO IS BRING ME THAT BABY!
I HAVE AN IDEA!
FLOP!
WAAAAH!
ASTERIX, SUPPOSE I GAVE HIM JUST ONE TINY DROP OF MAGIC POTION, MAYBE HE'D...
YOU'LL DO NO SUCH THING! YOU TWO HAVE CREATED ENOUGH HAVOC ALREADY!!!
ALL RIGHT, ALL RIGHT, I GET THE IDEA! MUSTN'T TREAT THIS PLACE LIKE HOME, MUST WE, DOGMATIX?
WAAAAH!
!
WAAAAH!
HEY... HE'S LEFT ME HOLDING THE BABY! OH, VERY CLEVER, MISTER OBELIX!

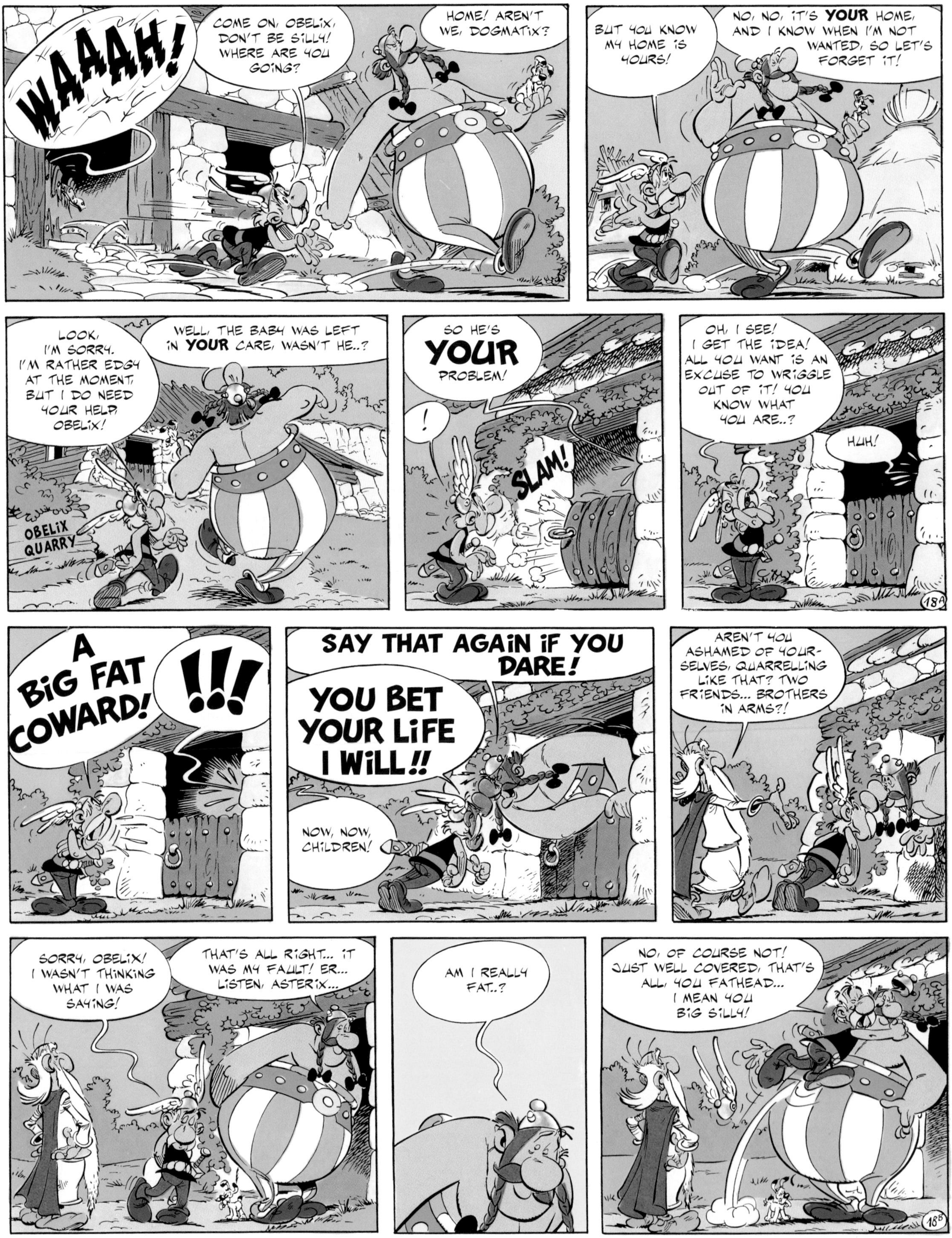
WAAAH!
COME ON, OBELIX, DON'T BE SILLY! WHERE ARE YOU GOING?
HOME! AREN'T WE, DOGMATIX?
BUT YOU KNOW MY HOME IS YOURS!
NO, NO, IT'S YOUR HOME, AND I KNOW WHEN I'M NOT WANTED, SO LET'S FORGET IT!
LOOK, I'M SORRY. I'M RATHER EDGY AT THE MOMENT, BUT I DO NEED YOUR HELP, OBELIX!
WELL, THE BABY WAS LEFT IN YOUR CARE, WASN'T HE..?
OBELIX QUARRY
SO HE'S YOUR PROBLEM!
!
SLAM!
OH, I SEE! I GET THE IDEA! ALL YOU WANT IS AN EXCUSE TO WRIGGLE OUT OF IT! YOU KNOW WHAT YOU ARE..?
HUH!
18A
A BIG FAT COWARD!
!!!
SAY THAT AGAIN IF YOU DARE!
YOU BET YOUR LIFE I WILL!!
NOW, NOW, CHILDREN!
AREN'T YOU ASHAMED OF YOURSELVES, QUARRELLING LIKE THAT? TWO FRIENDS... BROTHERS IN ARMS?!
SORRY, OBELIX! I WASN'T THINKING WHAT I WAS SAYING!
THAT'S ALL RIGHT... IT WAS MY FAULT! ER... LISTEN, ASTERIX...
AM I REALLY FAT..?
NO, OF COURSE NOT! JUST WELL COVERED, THAT'S ALL, YOU FATHEAD... I MEAN YOU BIG SILLY!
18B

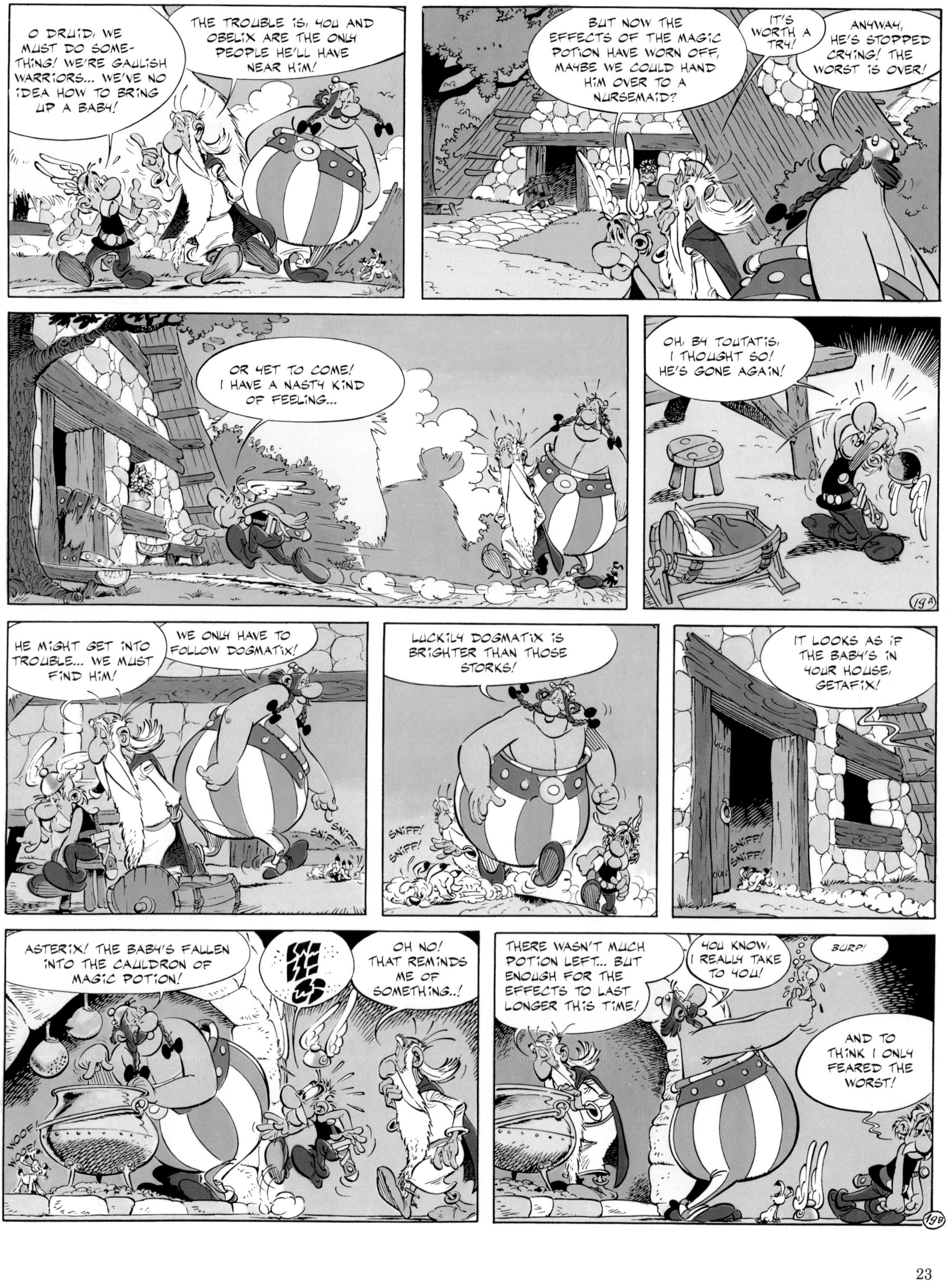
O DRUID, WE MUST DO SOMETHING! WE'RE GAULISH WARRIORS... WE'VE NO IDEA HOW TO BRING UP A BABY!
THE TROUBLE IS, YOU AND OBELIX ARE THE ONLY PEOPLE HE'LL HAVE NEAR HIM!
BUT NOW THE EFFECTS OF THE MAGIC POTION HAVE WORN OFF, MAYBE WE COULD HAND HIM OVER TO A NURSEMAID?
IT'S WORTH A TRY!
ANYWAY, HE'S STOPPED CRYING! THE WORST IS OVER!
OR YET TO COME! I HAVE A NASTY KIND OF FEELING...
OH, BY TOUTATIS, I THOUGHT SO! HE'S GONE AGAIN!
19A
HE MIGHT GET INTO TROUBLE... WE MUST FIND HIM!
WE ONLY HAVE TO FOLLOW DOGMATIX!
SNIFF! SNIFF!
LUCKILY DOGMATIX IS BRIGHTER THAN THOSE STORKS!
SNIFF! SNIFF!
IT LOOKS AS IF THE BABY'S IN YOUR HOUSE, GETAFIX!
SNIFF! SNIFF!
ASTERIX! THE BABY'S FALLEN INTO THE CAULDRON OF MAGIC POTION!
WOOF! WOOF!
OH NO! THAT REMINDS ME OF SOMETHING..!
THERE WASN'T MUCH POTION LEFT... BUT ENOUGH FOR THE EFFECTS TO LAST LONGER THIS TIME!
YOU KNOW, I REALLY TAKE TO YOU!
BURP!
AND TO THINK I ONLY FEARED THE WORST!
19B

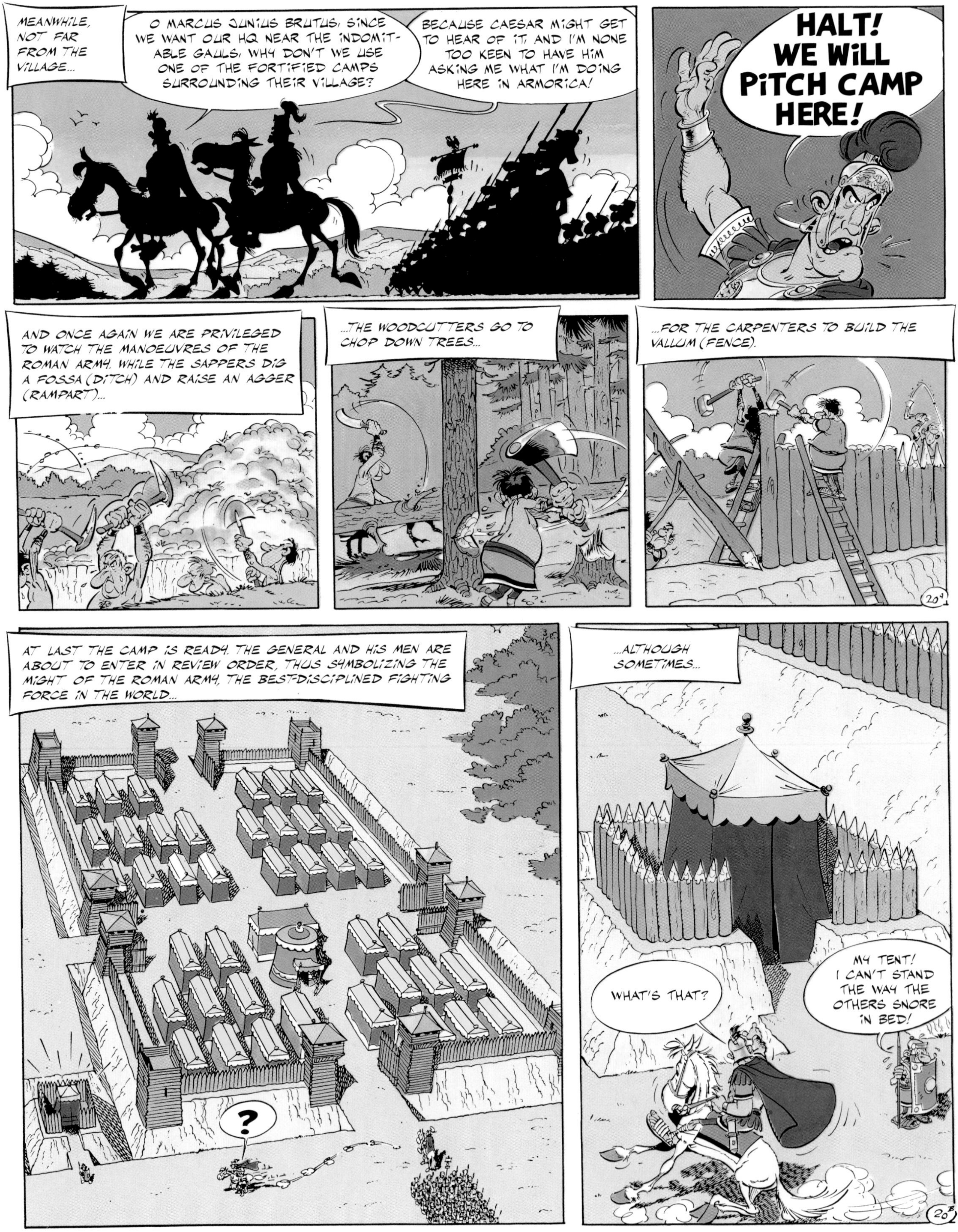
MEANWHILE, NOT FAR FROM THE VILLAGE...
O MARCUS JUNIUS BRUTUS, SINCE WE WANT OUR HQ NEAR THE INDOMITABLE GAULS, WHY DON'T WE USE ONE OF THE FORTIFIED CAMPS SURROUNDING THEIR VILLAGE?
BECAUSE CAESAR MIGHT GET TO HEAR OF IT, AND I'M NONE TOO KEEN TO HAVE HIM ASKING ME WHAT I'M DOING HERE IN ARMORICA!
HALT! WE WILL PITCH CAMP HERE!
AND ONCE AGAIN WE ARE PRIVILEGED TO WATCH THE MANOEUVRES OF THE ROMAN ARMY. WHILE THE SAPPERS DIG A FOSSA (DITCH) AND RAISE AN AGGER (RAMPART)...
...THE WOODCUTTERS GO TO CHOP DOWN TREES...
...FOR THE CARPENTERS TO BUILD THE VALLUM (FENCE).
AT LAST THE CAMP IS READY. THE GENERAL AND HIS MEN ARE ABOUT TO ENTER IN REVIEW ORDER, THUS SYMBOLIZING THE MIGHT OF THE ROMAN ARMY, THE BEST-DISCIPLINED FIGHTING FORCE IN THE WORLD...
?
...ALTHOUGH SOMETIMES...
WHAT'S THAT?
MY TENT! I CAN'T STAND THE WAY THE OTHERS SNORE IN BED!

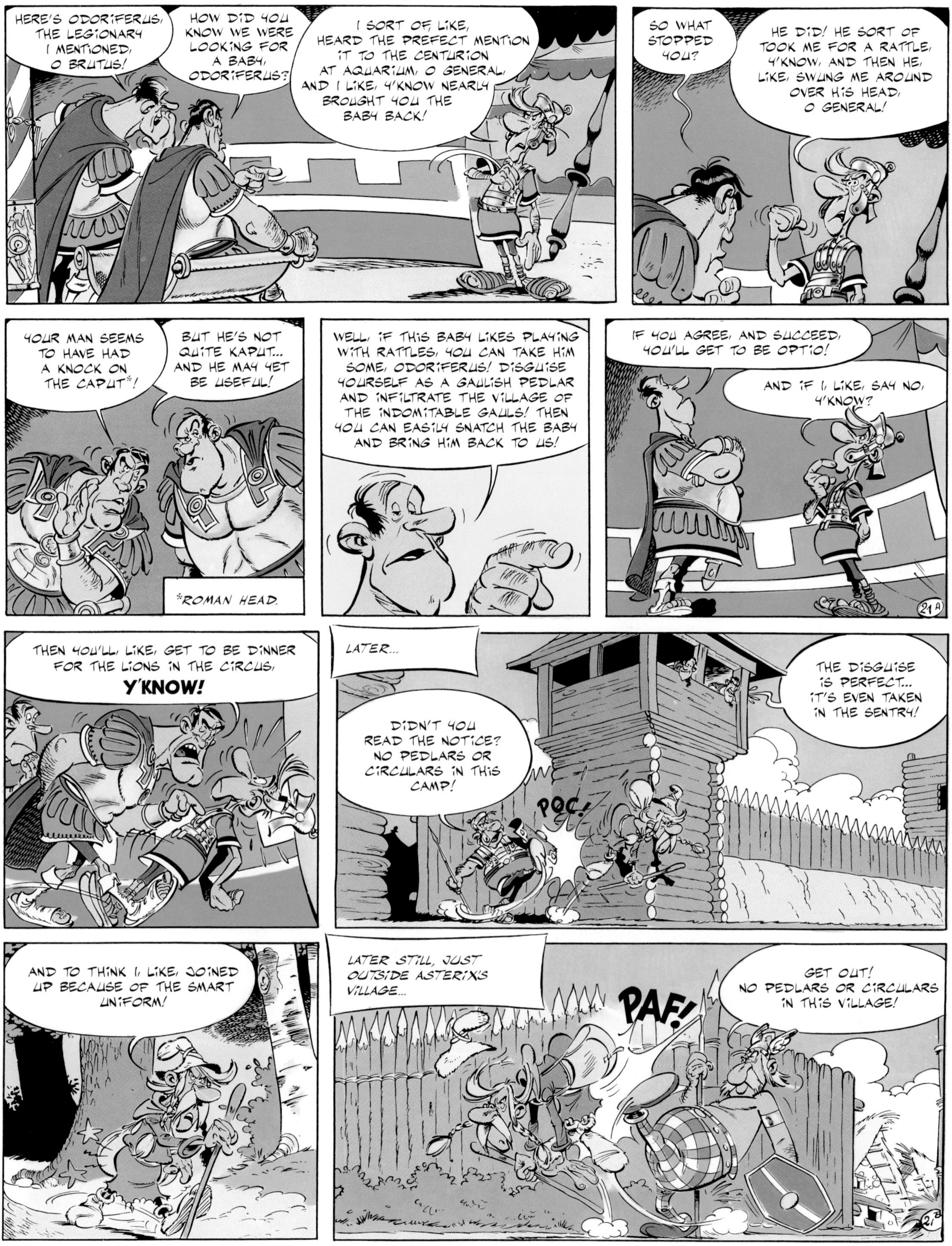
HERE'S ODORIFERUS, THE LEGIONARY I MENTIONED, O BRUTUS!
HOW DID YOU KNOW WE WERE LOOKING FOR A BABY, ODORIFERUS?
I SORT OF, LIKE, HEARD THE PREFECT MENTION IT TO THE CENTURION AT AQUARIUM, O GENERAL, AND I LIKE, Y'KNOW NEARLY BROUGHT YOU THE BABY BACK!
SO WHAT STOPPED YOU?
HE DID! HE SORT OF TOOK ME FOR A RATTLE, Y'KNOW, AND THEN HE, LIKE, SWUNG ME AROUND OVER HIS HEAD, O GENERAL!
YOUR MAN SEEMS TO HAVE HAD A KNOCK ON THE CAPUT*!
BUT HE'S NOT QUITE KAPUT... AND HE MAY YET BE USEFUL!
*ROMAN HEAD.
WELL, IF THIS BABY LIKES PLAYING WITH RATTLES, YOU CAN TAKE HIM SOME, ODORIFERUS! DISGUISE YOURSELF AS A GAULISH PEDLAR AND INFILTRATE THE VILLAGE OF THE INDOMITABLE GAULS! THEN YOU CAN EASILY SNATCH THE BABY AND BRING HIM BACK TO US!
IF YOU AGREE, AND SUCCEED, YOU'LL GET TO BE OPTIO!
AND IF I, LIKE, SAY NO, Y'KNOW?
21 A
THEN YOU'LL, LIKE, GET TO BE DINNER FOR THE LIONS IN THE CIRCUS, Y'KNOW!
LATER...
THE DISGUISE IS PERFECT... IT'S EVEN TAKEN IN THE SENTRY!
DIDN'T YOU READ THE NOTICE? NO PEDLARS OR CIRCULARS IN THIS CAMP!
POC!
AND TO THINK I, LIKE, JOINED UP BECAUSE OF THE SMART UNIFORM!
LATER STILL, JUST OUTSIDE ASTERIX'S VILLAGE...
PAF!
GET OUT! NO PEDLARS OR CIRCULARS IN THIS VILLAGE!
21 B

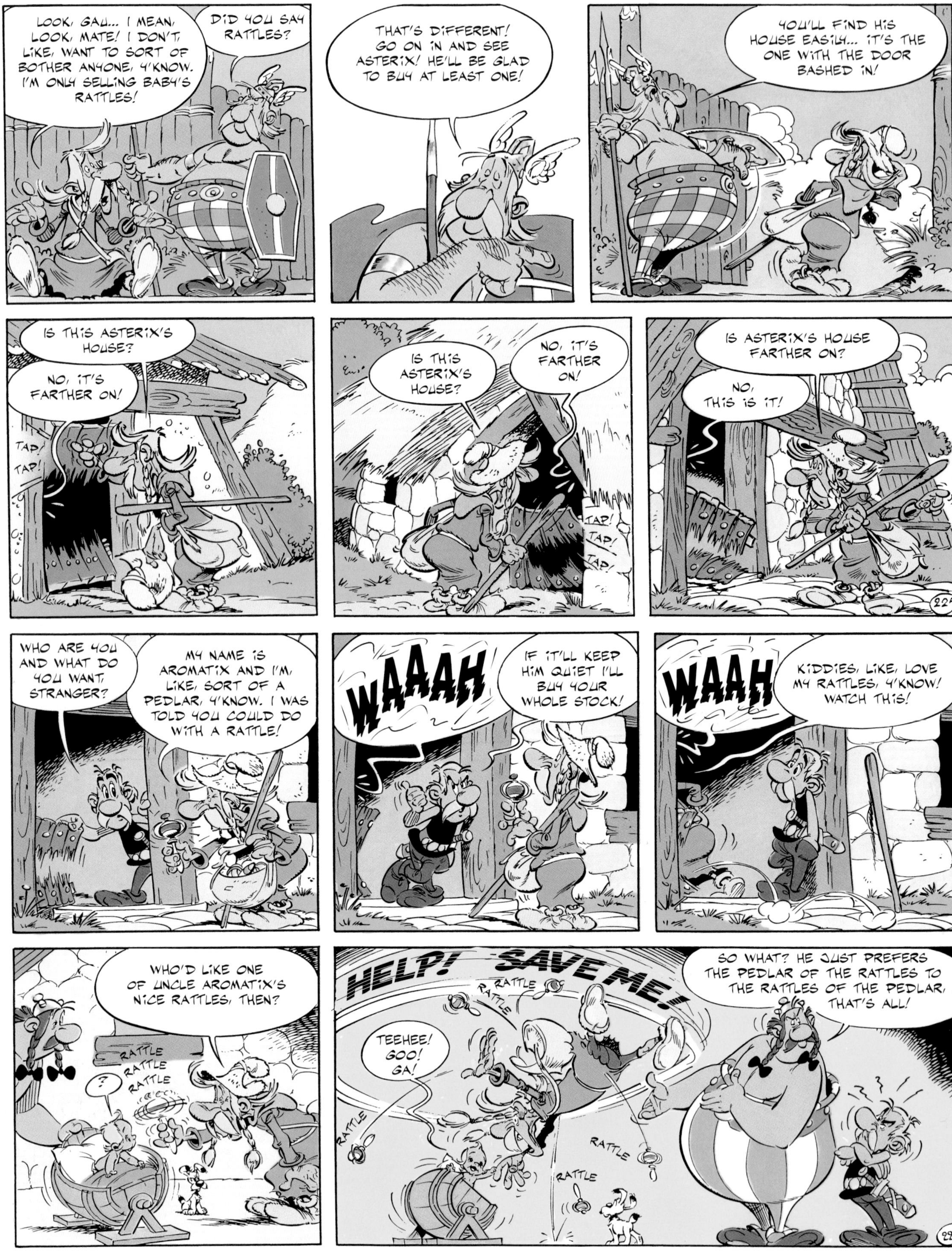
LOOK, GAU... I MEAN, LOOK, MATE! I DON'T, LIKE, WANT TO SORT OF BOTHER ANYONE, Y'KNOW. I'M ONLY SELLING BABY'S RATTLES!
DID YOU SAY RATTLES?
THAT'S DIFFERENT! GO ON IN AND SEE ASTERIX! HE'LL BE GLAD TO BUY AT LEAST ONE!
YOU'LL FIND HIS HOUSE EASILY... IT'S THE ONE WITH THE DOOR BASHED IN!
IS THIS ASTERIX'S HOUSE?
NO, IT'S FARTHER ON!
TAP! TAP!
IS THIS ASTERIX'S HOUSE?
NO, IT'S FARTHER ON!
TAP! TAP! TAP!
IS ASTERIX'S HOUSE FARTHER ON?
NO, THIS IS IT!
22A
WHO ARE YOU AND WHAT DO YOU WANT, STRANGER?
MY NAME IS AROMATIX AND I'M, LIKE, SORT OF A PEDLAR, Y'KNOW. I WAS TOLD YOU COULD DO WITH A RATTLE!
WAAAH
IF IT'LL KEEP HIM QUIET I'LL BUY YOUR WHOLE STOCK!
WAAH
KIDDIES, LIKE, LOVE MY RATTLES, Y'KNOW! WATCH THIS!
WHO'D LIKE ONE OF UNCLE AROMATIX'S NICE RATTLES, THEN?
RATTLE RATTLE RATTLE
?
HELP! SAVE ME!
RATTLE RATTLE
SO WHAT? HE JUST PREFERS THE PEDLAR OF THE RATTLES TO THE RATTLES OF THE PEDLAR, THAT'S ALL!
TEEHEE! GOO! GA!
RATTLE
RATTLE
RATTLE
22B

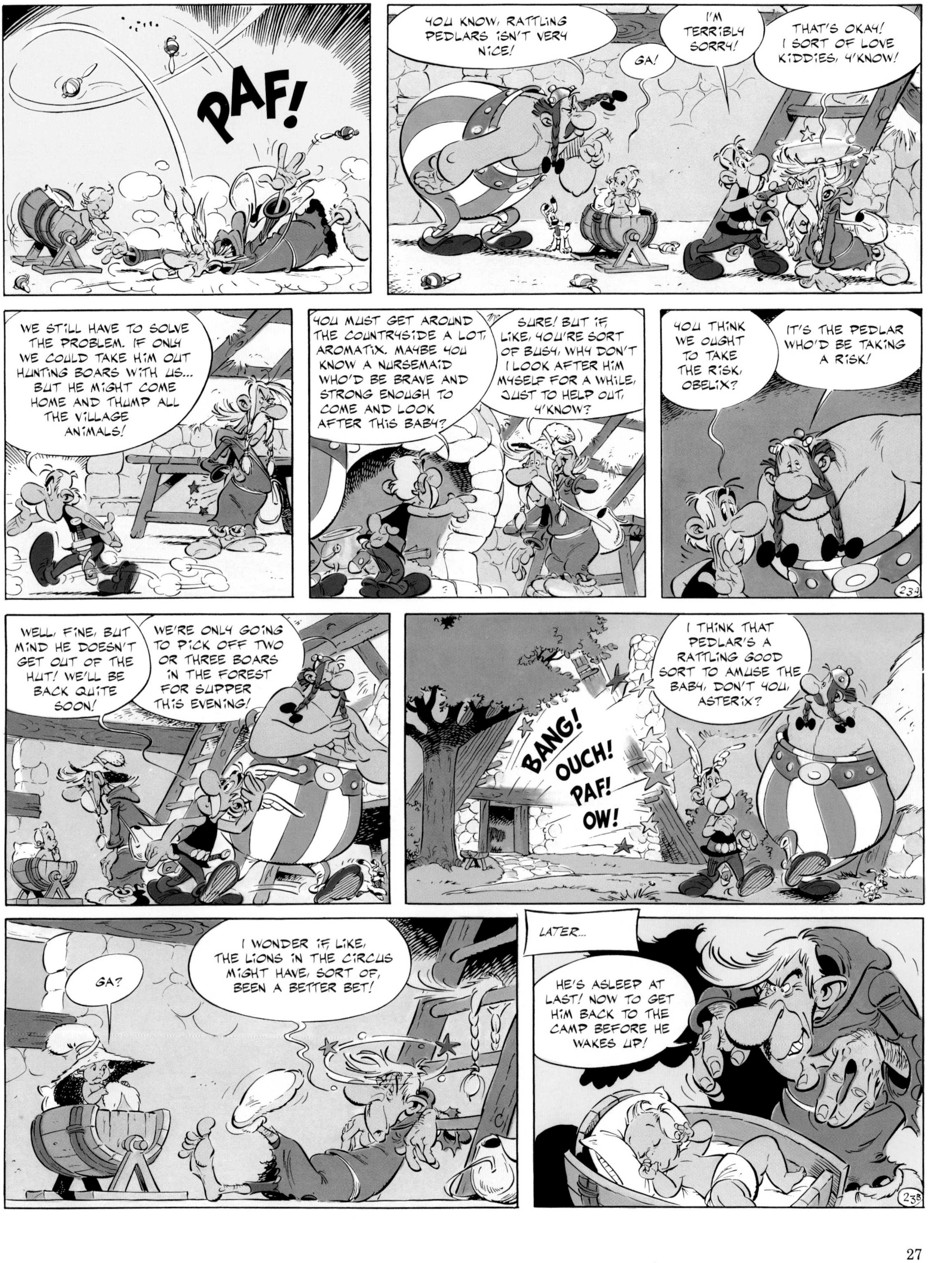
PAF!
YOU KNOW, RATTLING PEDLARS ISN'T VERY NICE!
GA!
I'M TERRIBLY SORRY!
THAT'S OKAY! I SORT OF LOVE KIDDIES, Y'KNOW!
WE STILL HAVE TO SOLVE THE PROBLEM. IF ONLY WE COULD TAKE HIM OUT HUNTING BOARS WITH US... BUT HE MIGHT COME HOME AND THUMP ALL THE VILLAGE ANIMALS!
YOU MUST GET AROUND THE COUNTRYSIDE A LOT, AROMATIX. MAYBE YOU KNOW A NURSEMAID WHO'D BE BRAVE AND STRONG ENOUGH TO COME AND LOOK AFTER THIS BABY?
SURE! BUT IF, LIKE, YOU'RE SORT OF BUSY, WHY DON'T I LOOK AFTER HIM MYSELF FOR A WHILE, JUST TO HELP OUT, Y'KNOW?
YOU THINK WE OUGHT TO TAKE THE RISK, OBELIX?
IT'S THE PEDLAR WHO'D BE TAKING A RISK!
WELL, FINE, BUT MIND HE DOESN'T GET OUT OF THE HUT! WE'LL BE BACK QUITE SOON!
WE'RE ONLY GOING TO PICK OFF TWO OR THREE BOARS IN THE FOREST FOR SUPPER THIS EVENING!
BANG!
OUCH!
PAF!
OW!
I THINK THAT PEDLAR'S A RATTLING GOOD SORT TO AMUSE THE BABY, DON'T YOU, ASTERIX?
GA?
I WONDER IF, LIKE, THE LIONS IN THE CIRCUS MIGHT HAVE, SORT OF, BEEN A BETTER BET!
LATER...
HE'S ASLEEP AT LAST! NOW TO GET HIM BACK TO THE CAMP BEFORE HE WAKES UP!

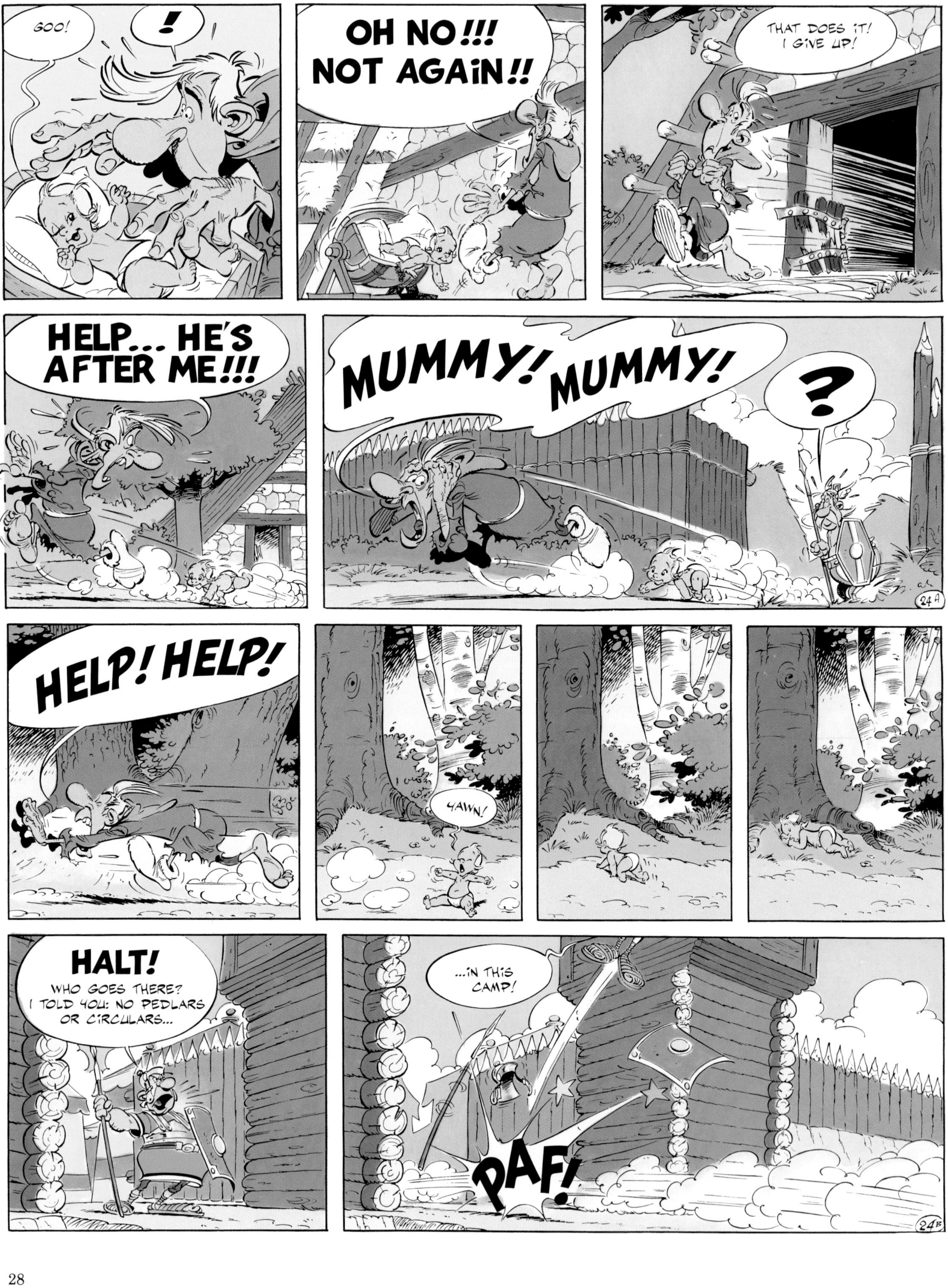

GOO!
!
OH NO!!! NOT AGAIN!!
THAT DOES IT! I GIVE UP!
HELP... HE'S AFTER ME!!!
MUMMY! MUMMY!
?
24A
HELP! HELP!
YAWN!
HALT! WHO GOES THERE? I TOLD YOU: NO PEDLARS OR CIRCULARS...
...IN THIS CAMP!
PAF!
24B

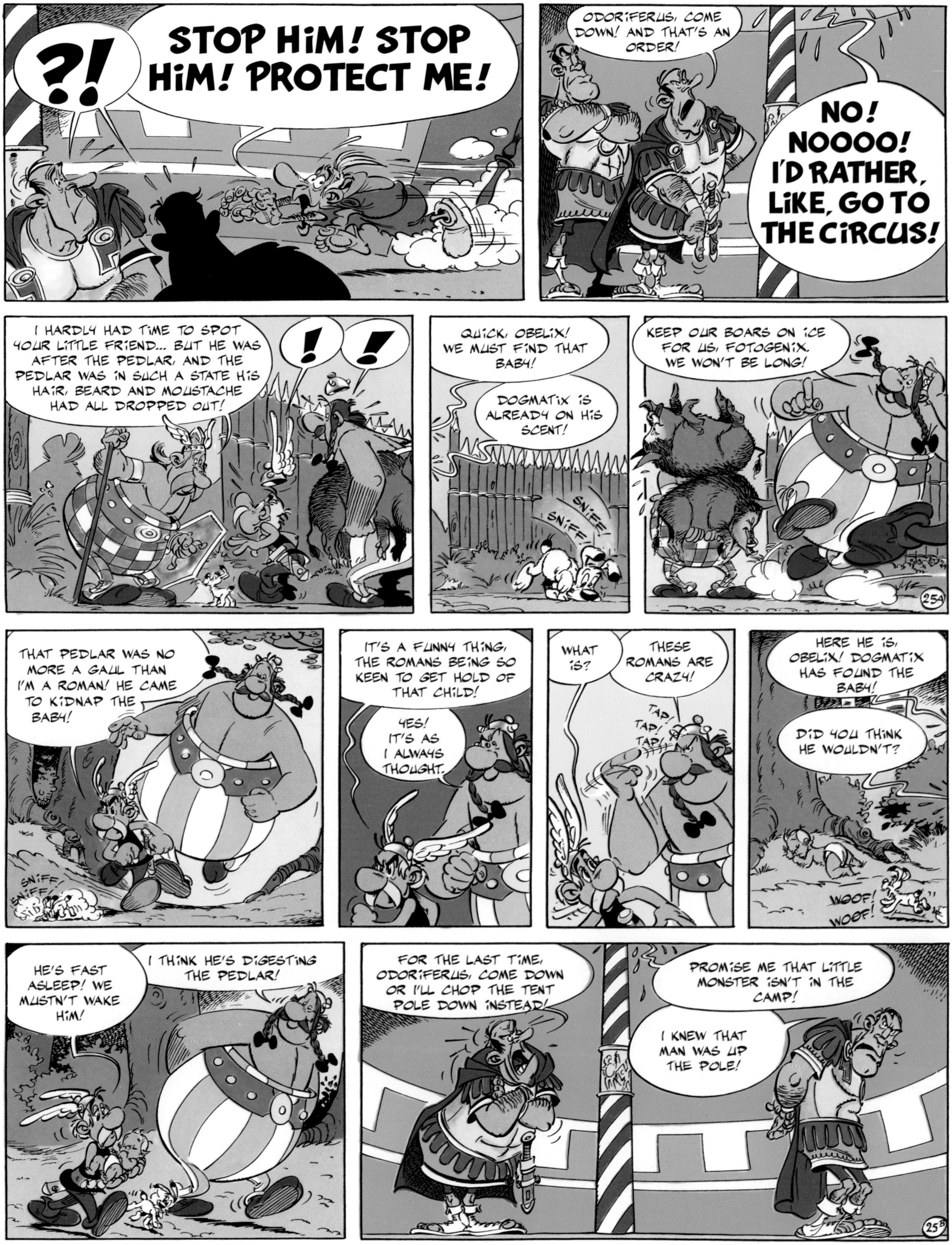
?!
STOP HIM! STOP HIM! PROTECT ME!
ODORIFERUS, COME DOWN! AND THAT'S AN ORDER!
NO! NOOOO! I'D RATHER, LIKE, GO TO THE CIRCUS!
I HARDLY HAD TIME TO SPOT YOUR LITTLE FRIEND... BUT HE WAS AFTER THE PEDLAR, AND THE PEDLAR WAS IN SUCH A STATE HIS HAIR, BEARD AND MOUSTACHE HAD ALL DROPPED OUT!
!
!
QUICK, OBELIX! WE MUST FIND THAT BABY!
DOGMATIX IS ALREADY ON HIS SCENT!
SNIFF SNIFF
KEEP OUR BOARS ON ICE FOR US, FOTOGENIX. WE WON'T BE LONG!
THAT PEDLAR WAS NO MORE A GAUL THAN I'M A ROMAN! HE CAME TO KIDNAP THE BABY!
SNIFF SNIFF
IT'S A FUNNY THING, THE ROMANS BEING SO KEEN TO GET HOLD OF THAT CHILD!
YES! IT'S AS I ALWAYS THOUGHT.
WHAT IS?
THESE ROMANS ARE CRAZY!
TAP! TAP! TAP!
HERE HE IS, OBELIX! DOGMATIX HAS FOUND THE BABY!
DID YOU THINK HE WOULDN'T?
WOOF! WOOF!
HE'S FAST ASLEEP! WE MUSTN'T WAKE HIM!
I THINK HE'S DIGESTING THE PEDLAR!
FOR THE LAST TIME, ODORIFERUS, COME DOWN OR I'LL CHOP THE TENT POLE DOWN INSTEAD!
PROMISE ME THAT LITTLE MONSTER ISN'T IN THE CAMP!
I KNEW THAT MAN WAS UP THE POLE!

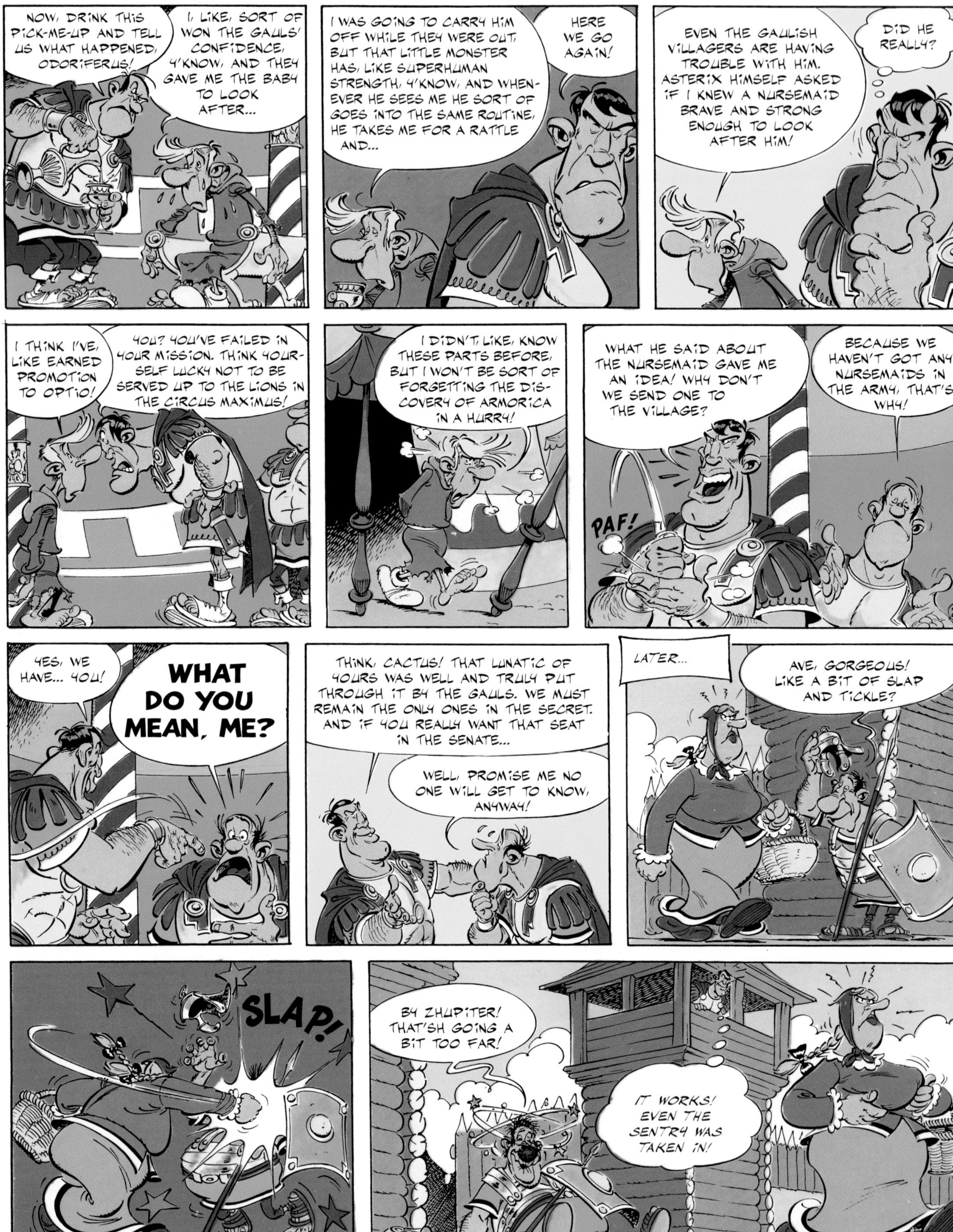
NOW, DRINK THIS PICK-ME-UP AND TELL US WHAT HAPPENED, ODORIFERUS!
I, LIKE, SORT OF WON THE GAULS' CONFIDENCE, Y'KNOW, AND THEY GAVE ME THE BABY TO LOOK AFTER...
I WAS GOING TO CARRY HIM OFF WHILE THEY WERE OUT, BUT THAT LITTLE MONSTER HAS, LIKE SUPERHUMAN STRENGTH, Y'KNOW, AND WHENEVER HE SEES ME HE SORT OF GOES INTO THE SAME ROUTINE, HE TAKES ME FOR A RATTLE AND...
HERE WE GO AGAIN!
EVEN THE GAULISH VILLAGERS ARE HAVING TROUBLE WITH HIM. ASTERIX HIMSELF ASKED IF I KNEW A NURSEMAID BRAVE AND STRONG ENOUGH TO LOOK AFTER HIM!
DID HE REALLY?
I THINK I'VE, LIKE EARNED PROMOTION TO OPTIO!
YOU? YOU'VE FAILED IN YOUR MISSION. THINK YOURSELF LUCKY NOT TO BE SERVED UP TO THE LIONS IN THE CIRCUS MAXIMUS!
I DIDN'T, LIKE, KNOW THESE PARTS BEFORE, BUT I WON'T BE SORT OF FORGETTING THE DISCOVERY OF ARMORICA IN A HURRY!
WHAT HE SAID ABOUT THE NURSEMAID GAVE ME AN IDEA! WHY DON'T WE SEND ONE TO THE VILLAGE?
BECAUSE WE HAVEN'T GOT ANY NURSEMAIDS IN THE ARMY, THAT'S WHY!
PAF!
YES, WE HAVE... YOU!
WHAT DO YOU MEAN, ME?
THINK, CACTUS! THAT LUNATIC OF YOURS WAS WELL AND TRULY PUT THROUGH IT BY THE GAULS. WE MUST REMAIN THE ONLY ONES IN THE SECRET. AND IF YOU REALLY WANT THAT SEAT IN THE SENATE...
WELL, PROMISE ME NO ONE WILL GET TO KNOW, ANYWAY!
LATER...
AVE, GORGEOUS! LIKE A BIT OF SLAP AND TICKLE?
SLAP!
BY ZHUPITER! THAT'SH GOING A BIT TOO FAR!
IT WORKS! EVEN THE SENTRY WAS TAKEN IN!

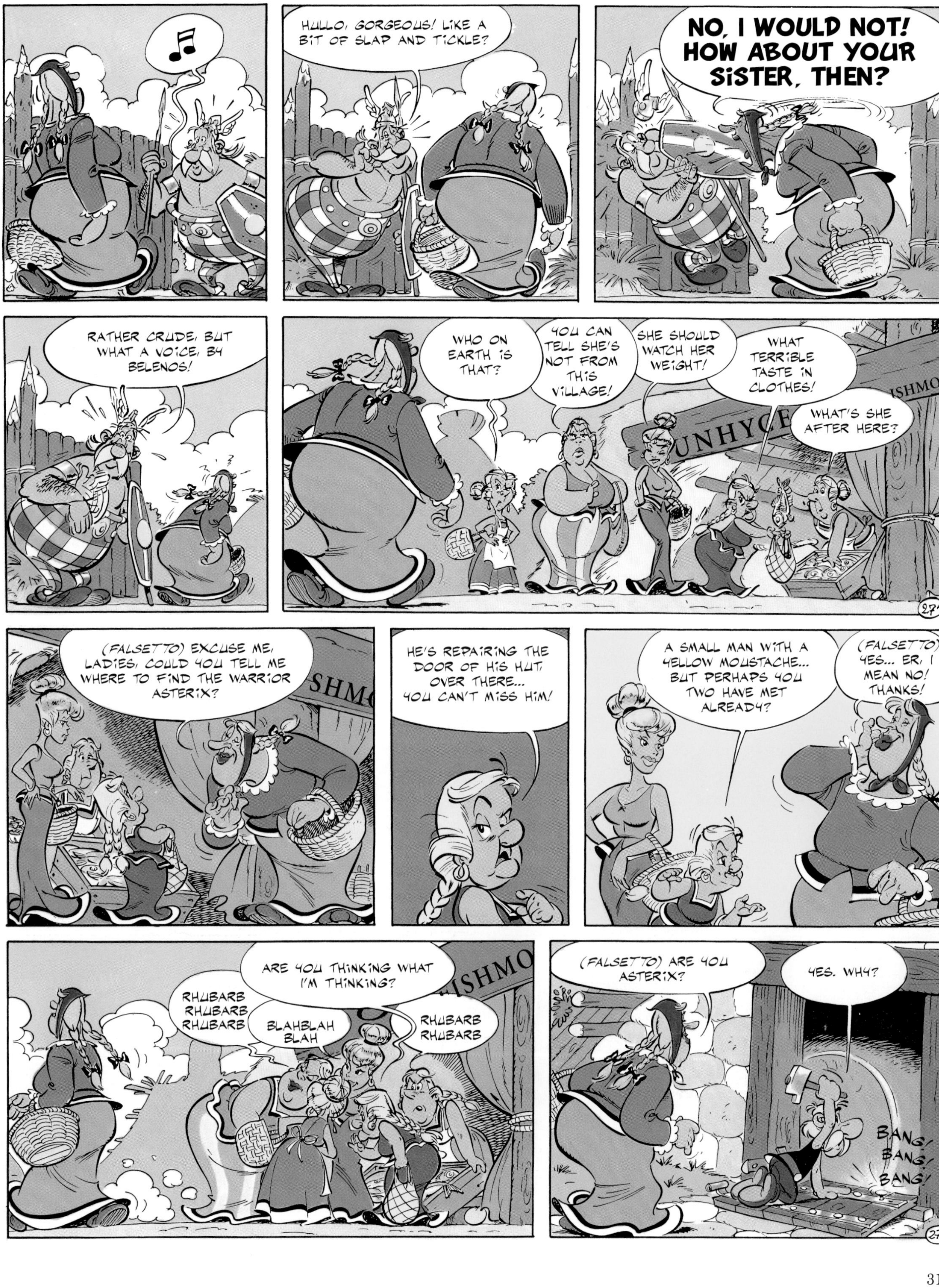

HULLO, GORGEOUS! LIKE A BIT OF SLAP AND TICKLE?
NO, I WOULD NOT! HOW ABOUT YOUR SISTER, THEN?
RATHER CRUDE, BUT WHAT A VOICE, BY BELENOS!
WHO ON EARTH IS THAT?
YOU CAN TELL SHE'S NOT FROM THIS VILLAGE!
SHE SHOULD WATCH HER WEIGHT!
WHAT TERRIBLE TASTE IN CLOTHES!
WHAT'S SHE AFTER HERE?
UNHYGE
ISHMO
27A
(FALSETTO) EXCUSE ME, LADIES, COULD YOU TELL ME WHERE TO FIND THE WARRIOR ASTERIX?
SHMO
HE'S REPAIRING THE DOOR OF HIS HUT, OVER THERE... YOU CAN'T MISS HIM!
A SMALL MAN WITH A YELLOW MOUSTACHE... BUT PERHAPS YOU TWO HAVE MET ALREADY?
(FALSETTO) YES... ER, I MEAN NO! THANKS!
ARE YOU THINKING WHAT I'M THINKING?
RHUBARB RHUBARB RHUBARB
BLAHBLAH BLAH
RHUBARB RHUBARB
ISHMO
(FALSETTO) ARE YOU ASTERIX?
YES. WHY?
BANG! BANG! BANG!
27B

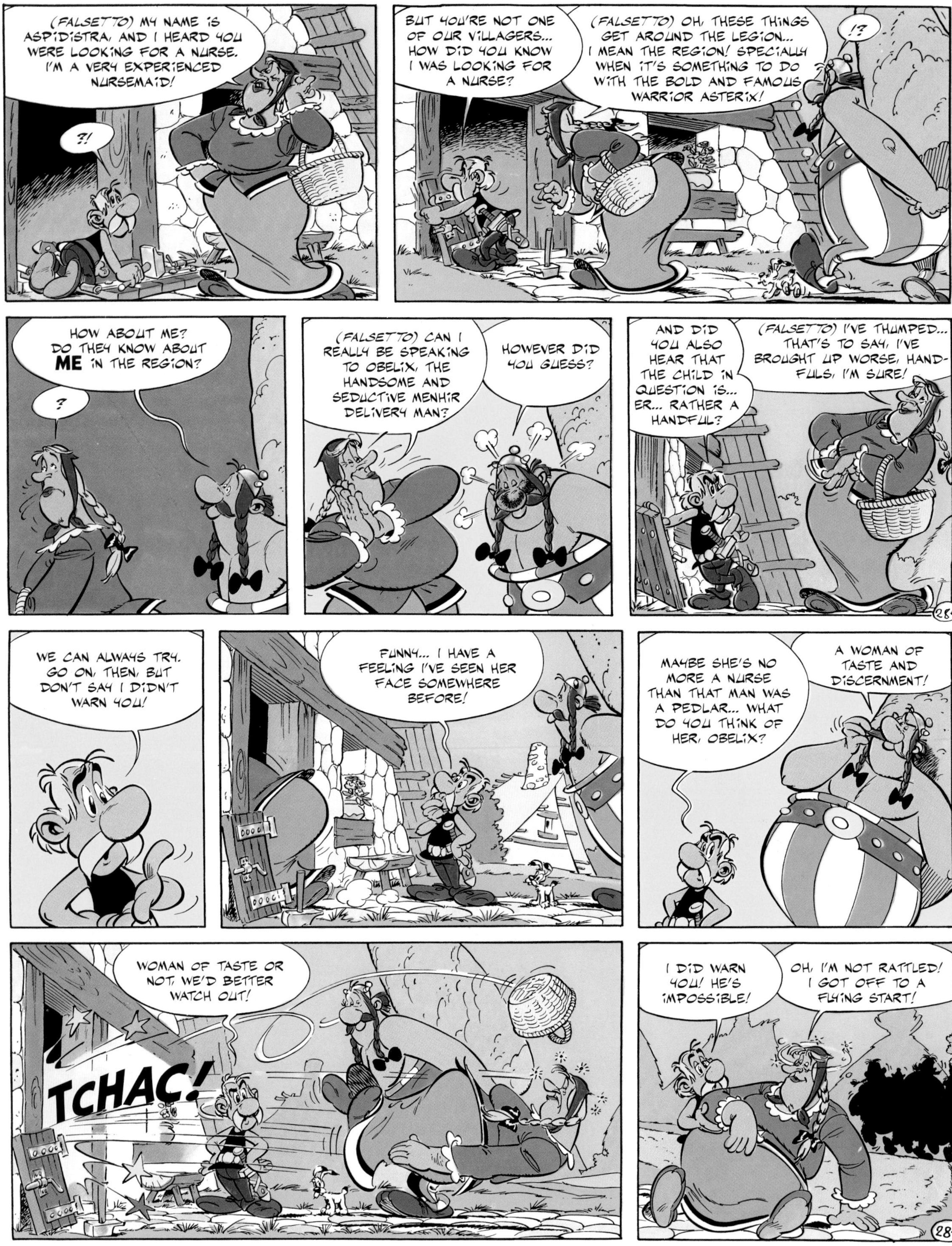
(FALSETTO) MY NAME IS ASPIDISTRA, AND I HEARD YOU WERE LOOKING FOR A NURSE. I'M A VERY EXPERIENCED NURSEMAID!
?!
BUT YOU'RE NOT ONE OF OUR VILLAGERS... HOW DID YOU KNOW I WAS LOOKING FOR A NURSE?
(FALSETTO) OH, THESE THINGS GET AROUND THE LEGION... I MEAN THE REGION! SPECIALLY WHEN IT'S SOMETHING TO DO WITH THE BOLD AND FAMOUS WARRIOR ASTERIX!
!?
HOW ABOUT ME? DO THEY KNOW ABOUT ME IN THE REGION?
?
(FALSETTO) CAN I REALLY BE SPEAKING TO OBELIX, THE HANDSOME AND SEDUCTIVE MENHIR DELIVERY MAN?
HOWEVER DID YOU GUESS?
AND DID YOU ALSO HEAR THAT THE CHILD IN QUESTION IS... ER... RATHER A HANDFUL?
(FALSETTO) I'VE THUMPED... THAT'S TO SAY, I'VE BROUGHT UP WORSE HANDFULS, I'M SURE!
WE CAN ALWAYS TRY. GO ON, THEN, BUT DON'T SAY I DIDN'T WARN YOU!
FUNNY... I HAVE A FEELING I'VE SEEN HER FACE SOMEWHERE BEFORE!
MAYBE SHE'S NO MORE A NURSE THAN THAT MAN WAS A PEDLAR... WHAT DO YOU THINK OF HER, OBELIX?
A WOMAN OF TASTE AND DISCERNMENT!
WOMAN OF TASTE OR NOT, WE'D BETTER WATCH OUT!
TCHAC!
I DID WARN YOU! HE'S IMPOSSIBLE!
OH, I'M NOT RATTLED! I GOT OFF TO A FLYING START!

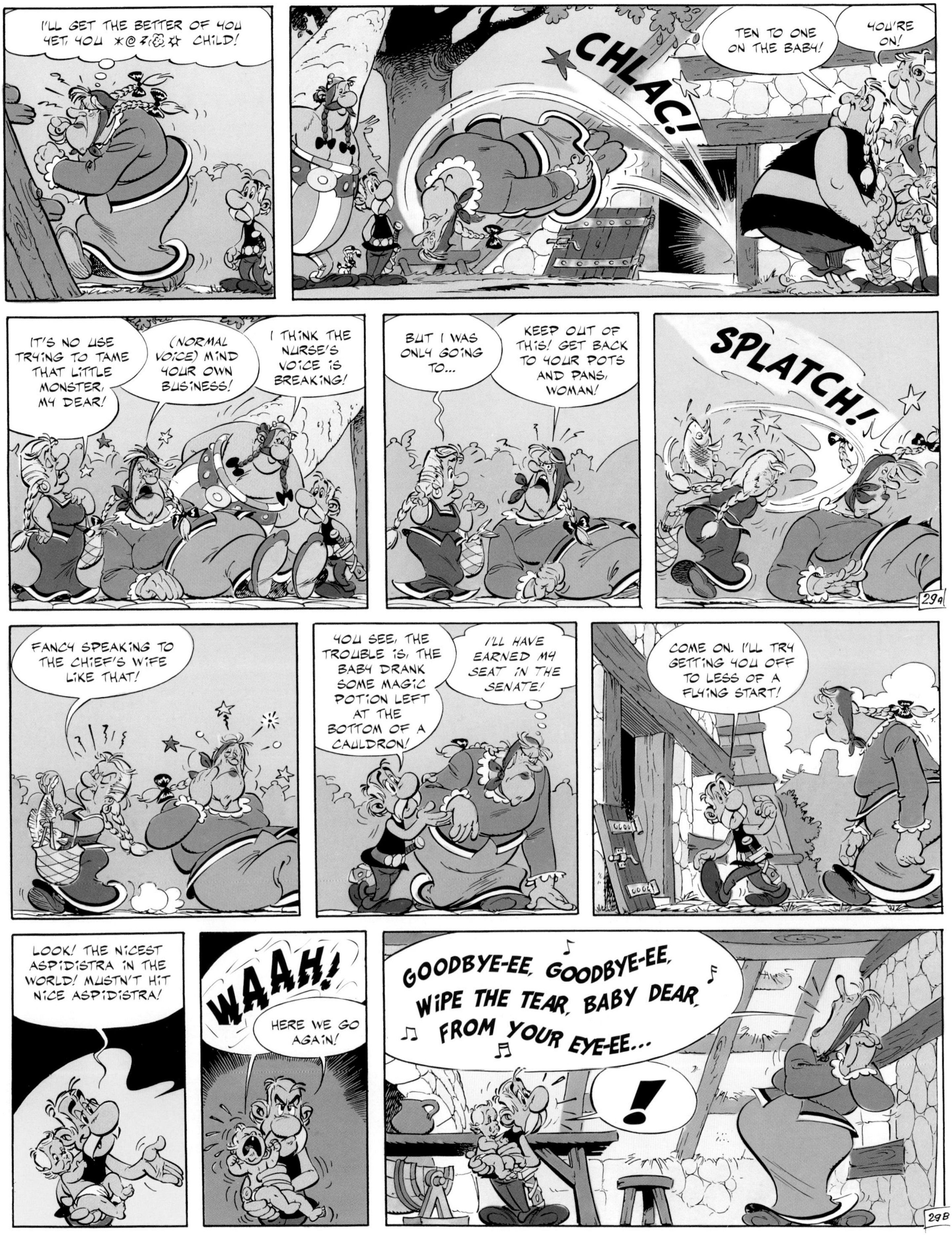
I'LL GET THE BETTER OF YOU YET, YOU *@✿☆ CHILD!
CHLAC!
TEN TO ONE ON THE BABY!
YOU'RE ON!
IT'S NO USE TRYING TO TAME THAT LITTLE MONSTER, MY DEAR!
(NORMAL VOICE) MIND YOUR OWN BUSINESS!
I THINK THE NURSE'S VOICE IS BREAKING!
BUT I WAS ONLY GOING TO...
KEEP OUT OF THIS! GET BACK TO YOUR POTS AND PANS, WOMAN!
SPLATCH!
29a
FANCY SPEAKING TO THE CHIEF'S WIFE LIKE THAT!
YOU SEE, THE TROUBLE IS, THE BABY DRANK SOME MAGIC POTION LEFT AT THE BOTTOM OF A CAULDRON!
I'LL HAVE EARNED MY SEAT IN THE SENATE!
COME ON. I'LL TRY GETTING YOU OFF TO LESS OF A FLYING START!
LOOK! THE NICEST ASPIDISTRA IN THE WORLD! MUSTN'T HIT NICE ASPIDISTRA!
WAAH!
HERE WE GO AGAIN!
GOODBYE-EE, GOODBYE-EE, WIPE THE TEAR, BABY DEAR, FROM YOUR EYE-EE...
!
29B

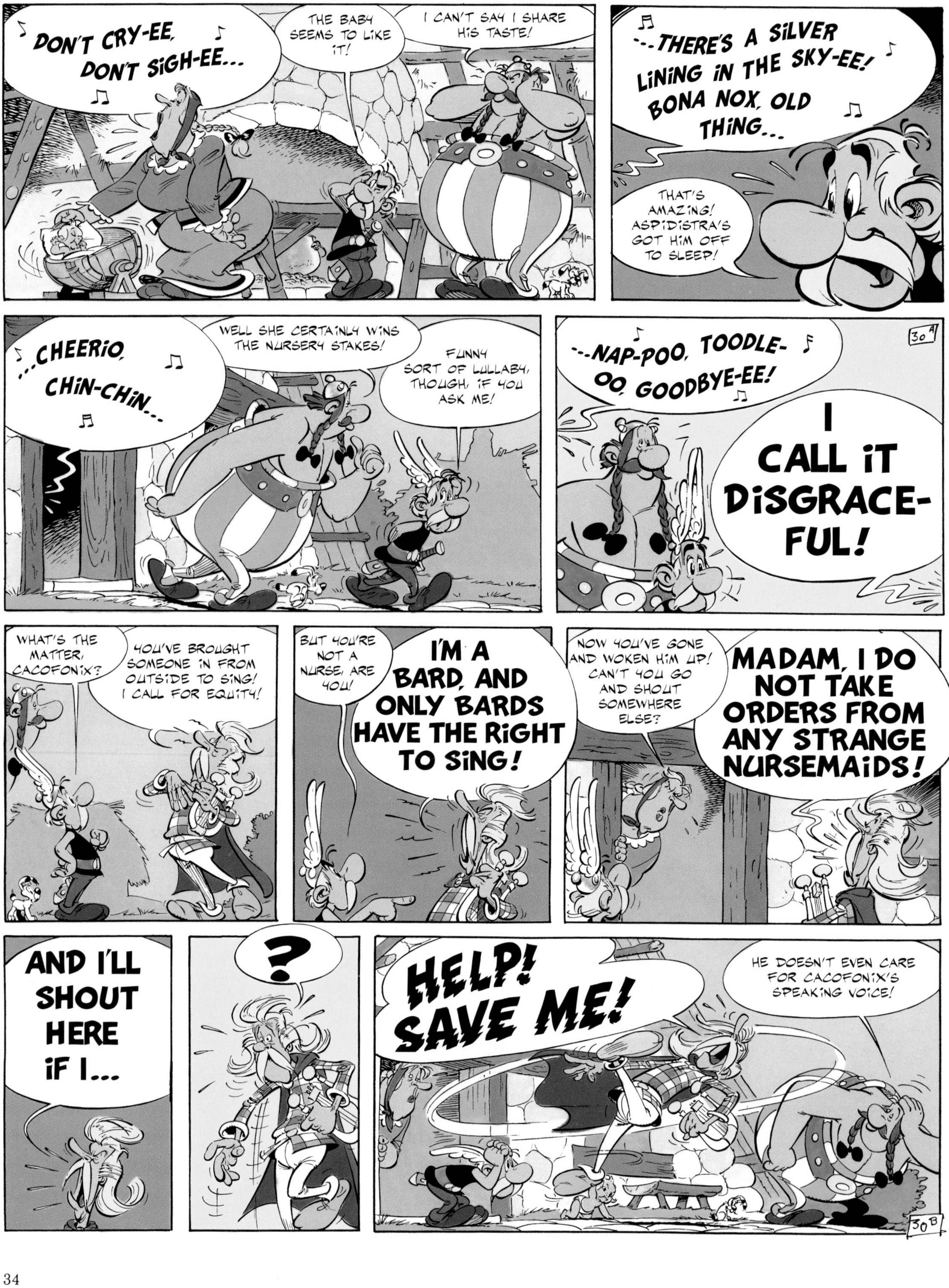

DON'T CRY-EE, DON'T SIGH-EE...
THE BABY SEEMS TO LIKE IT!
I CAN'T SAY I SHARE HIS TASTE!
...THERE'S A SILVER LINING IN THE SKY-EE! BONA NOX, OLD THING...
THAT'S AMAZING! ASPIDISTRA'S GOT HIM OFF TO SLEEP!
...CHEERIO, CHIN-CHIN...
WELL SHE CERTAINLY WINS THE NURSERY STAKES!
FUNNY SORT OF LULLABY, THOUGH, IF YOU ASK ME!
...NAP-POO, TOODLE-OO, GOODBYE-EE!
I CALL IT DISGRACE-FUL!
WHAT'S THE MATTER, CACOFONIX?
YOU'VE BROUGHT SOMEONE IN FROM OUTSIDE TO SING! I CALL FOR EQUITY!
BUT YOU'RE NOT A NURSE, ARE YOU!
I'M A BARD, AND ONLY BARDS HAVE THE RIGHT TO SING!
NOW YOU'VE GONE AND WOKEN HIM UP! CAN'T YOU GO AND SHOUT SOMEWHERE ELSE?
MADAM, I DO NOT TAKE ORDERS FROM ANY STRANGE NURSEMAIDS!
AND I'LL SHOUT HERE IF I...
?
HELP! SAVE ME!
HE DOESN'T EVEN CARE FOR CACOFONIX'S SPEAKING VOICE!

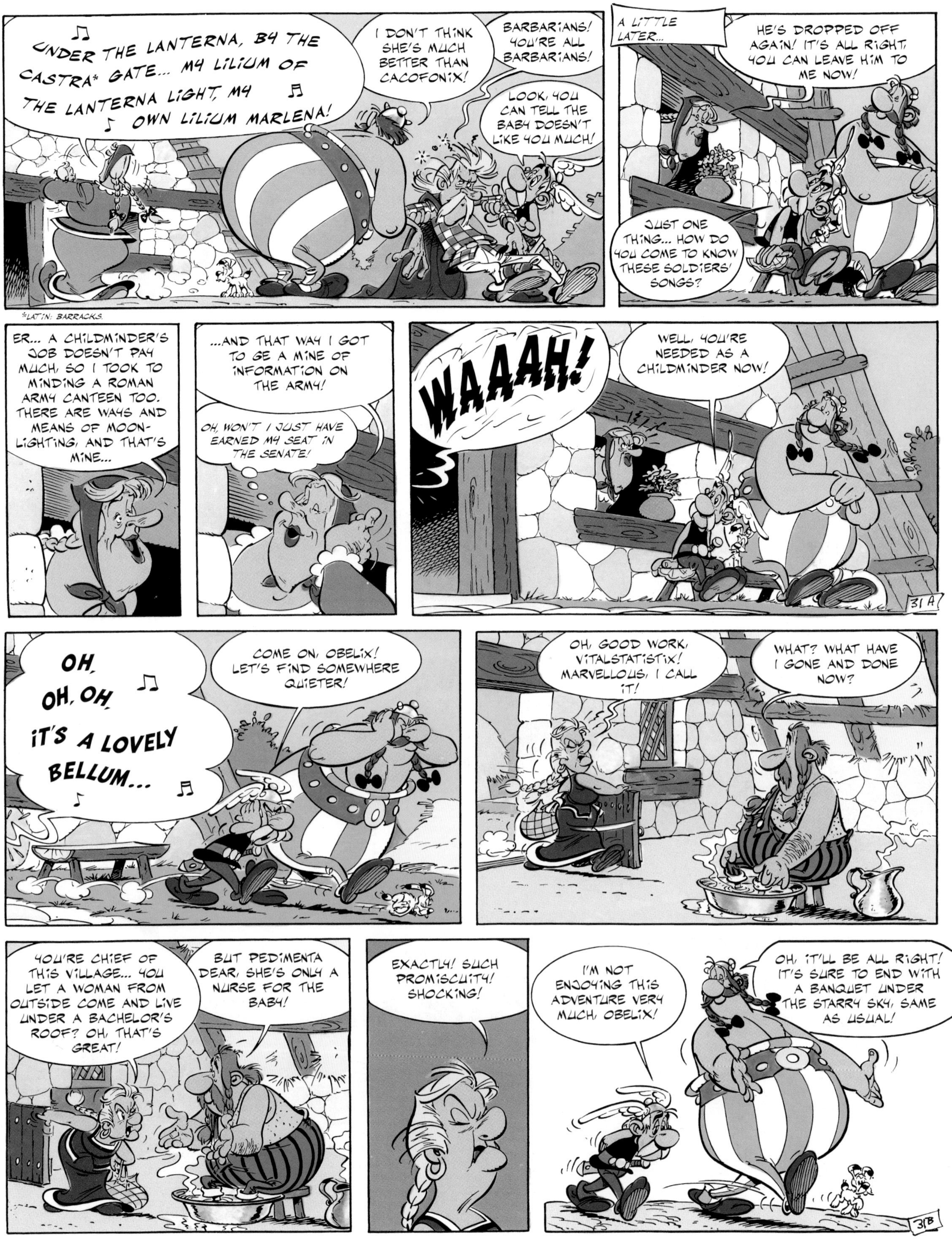
UNDER THE LANTERNA, BY THE CASTRA* GATE... MY LILIUM OF THE LANTERNA LIGHT, MY OWN LILIUM MARLENA!
I DON'T THINK SHE'S MUCH BETTER THAN CACOFONIX!
BARBARIANS! YOU'RE ALL BARBARIANS!
LOOK, YOU CAN TELL THE BABY DOESN'T LIKE YOU MUCH!
A LITTLE LATER...
HE'S DROPPED OFF AGAIN! IT'S ALL RIGHT, YOU CAN LEAVE HIM TO ME NOW!
JUST ONE THING... HOW DO YOU COME TO KNOW THESE SOLDIERS' SONGS?
*LATIN: BARRACKS.
ER... A CHILDMINDER'S JOB DOESN'T PAY MUCH, SO I TOOK TO MINDING A ROMAN ARMY CANTEEN TOO. THERE ARE WAYS AND MEANS OF MOON-LIGHTING, AND THAT'S MINE...
...AND THAT WAY I GOT TO GE A MINE OF INFORMATION ON THE ARMY!
OH, WON'T I JUST HAVE EARNED MY SEAT IN THE SENATE!
WAAAH!
WELL, YOU'RE NEEDED AS A CHILDMINDER NOW!
31 A
OH, OH, OH, IT'S A LOVELY BELLUM...
COME ON, OBELIX! LET'S FIND SOMEWHERE QUIETER!
OH, GOOD WORK, VITALSTATISTIX! MARVELLOUS, I CALL IT!
WHAT? WHAT HAVE I GONE AND DONE NOW?
YOU'RE CHIEF OF THIS VILLAGE... YOU LET A WOMAN FROM OUTSIDE COME AND LIVE UNDER A BACHELOR'S ROOF? OH, THAT'S GREAT!
BUT PEDIMENTA DEAR, SHE'S ONLY A NURSE FOR THE BABY!
EXACTLY! SUCH PROMISCUITY! SHOCKING!
I'M NOT ENJOYING THIS ADVENTURE VERY MUCH, OBELIX!
OH, IT'LL BE ALL RIGHT! IT'S SURE TO END WITH A BANQUET UNDER THE STARRY SKY, SAME AS USUAL!
31 B

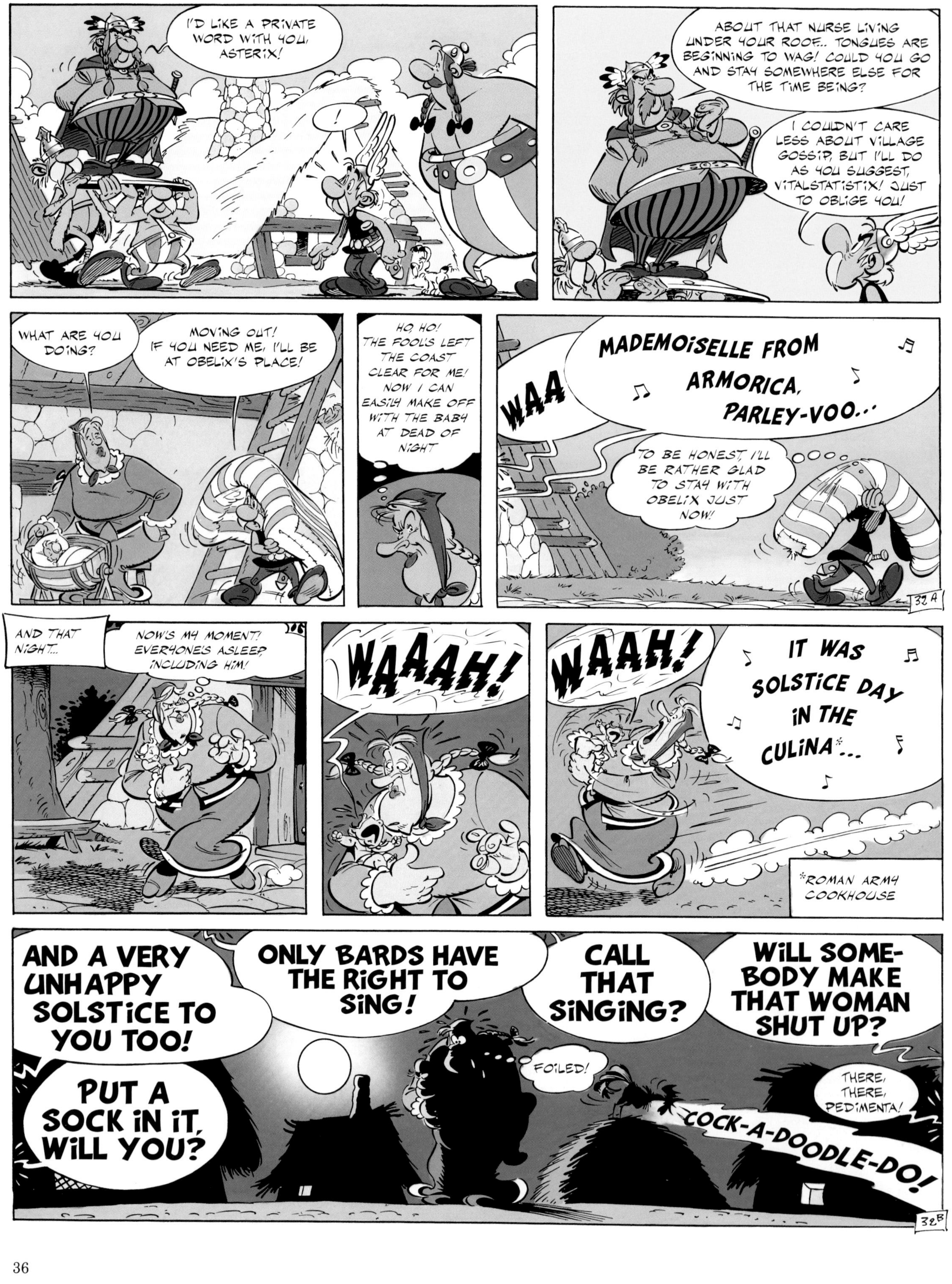
I'D LIKE A PRIVATE WORD WITH YOU, ASTERIX!
!
ABOUT THAT NURSE LIVING UNDER YOUR ROOF.. TONGUES ARE BEGINNING TO WAG! COULD YOU GO AND STAY SOMEWHERE ELSE FOR THE TIME BEING?
I COULDN'T CARE LESS ABOUT VILLAGE GOSSIP, BUT I'LL DO AS YOU SUGGEST, VITALSTATISTIX! JUST TO OBLIGE YOU!
WHAT ARE YOU DOING?
MOVING OUT! IF YOU NEED ME, I'LL BE AT OBELIX'S PLACE!
HO, HO! THE FOOL'S LEFT THE COAST CLEAR FOR ME! NOW I CAN EASILY MAKE OFF WITH THE BABY AT DEAD OF NIGHT
WAA
MADEMOISELLE FROM ARMORICA, PARLEY-VOO...
TO BE HONEST, I'LL BE RATHER GLAD TO STAY WITH OBELIX JUST NOW!
AND THAT NIGHT...
NOW'S MY MOMENT! EVERYONE'S ASLEEP, INCLUDING HIM!
WAAAH!
WAAH!
IT WAS SOLSTICE DAY IN THE CULINA*...
*ROMAN ARMY COOKHOUSE
AND A VERY UNHAPPY SOLSTICE TO YOU TOO!
ONLY BARDS HAVE THE RIGHT TO SING!
CALL THAT SINGING?
WILL SOMEBODY MAKE THAT WOMAN SHUT UP?
PUT A SOCK IN IT, WILL YOU?
FOILED!
THERE, THERE, PEDIMENTA!
COCK-A-DOODLE-DO!

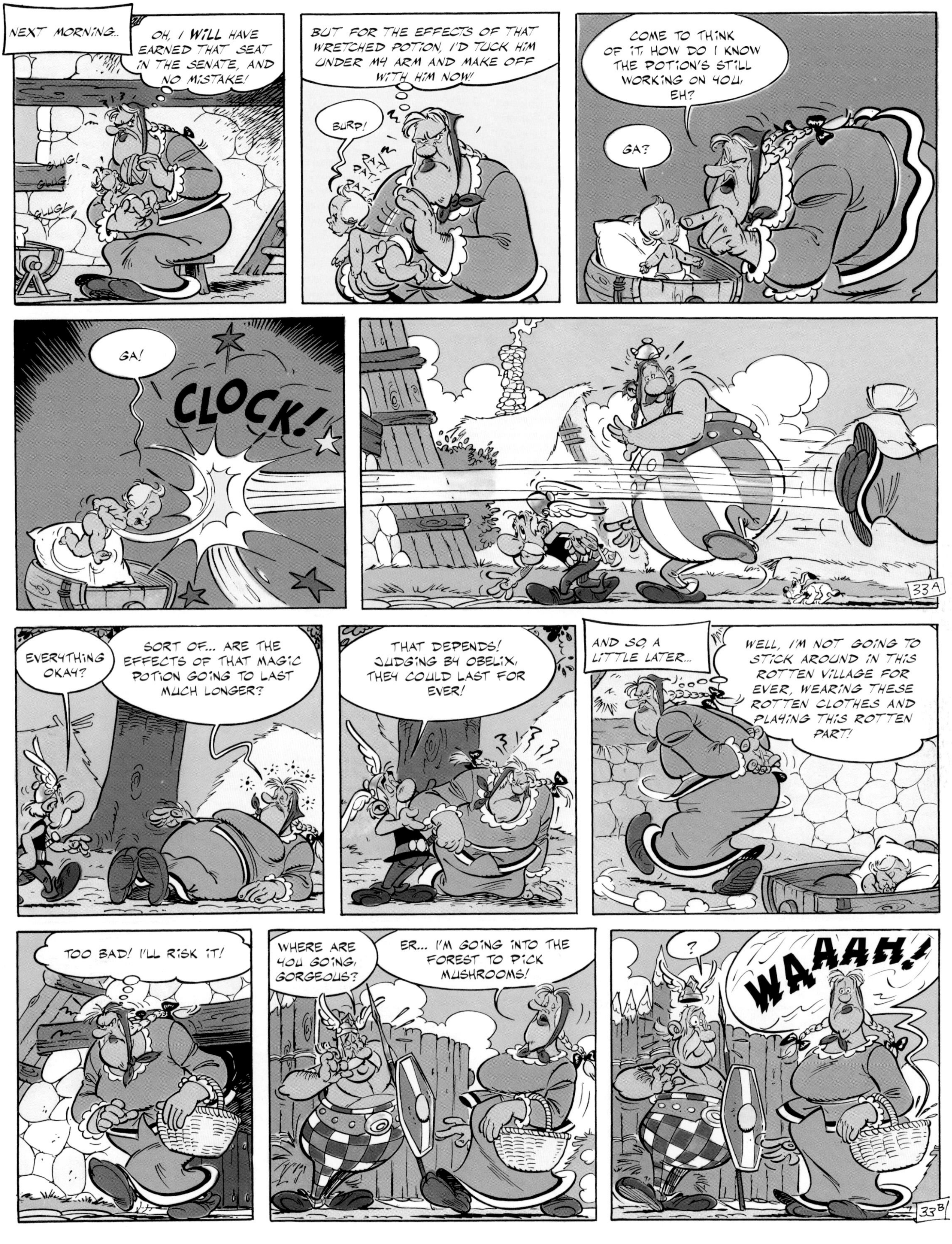
NEXT MORNING...
OH, I WILL HAVE EARNED THAT SEAT IN THE SENATE, AND NO MISTAKE!
GLUG!
GLUG!
GLUG!
BUT FOR THE EFFECTS OF THAT WRETCHED POTION, I'D TUCK HIM UNDER MY ARM AND MAKE OFF WITH HIM NOW!
BURP!
PAT PAT PAT
COME TO THINK OF IT, HOW DO I KNOW THE POTION'S STILL WORKING ON YOU, EH?
GA?
GA!
CLOCK!
EVERYTHING OKAY?
SORT OF... ARE THE EFFECTS OF THAT MAGIC POTION GOING TO LAST MUCH LONGER?
THAT DEPENDS! JUDGING BY OBELIX, THEY COULD LAST FOR EVER!
AND SO, A LITTLE LATER...
WELL, I'M NOT GOING TO STICK AROUND IN THIS ROTTEN VILLAGE FOR EVER, WEARING THESE ROTTEN CLOTHES AND PLAYING THIS ROTTEN PART!
TOO BAD! I'LL RISK IT!
WHERE ARE YOU GOING, GORGEOUS?
ER... I'M GOING INTO THE FOREST TO PICK MUSHROOMS!
?
WAAAH!

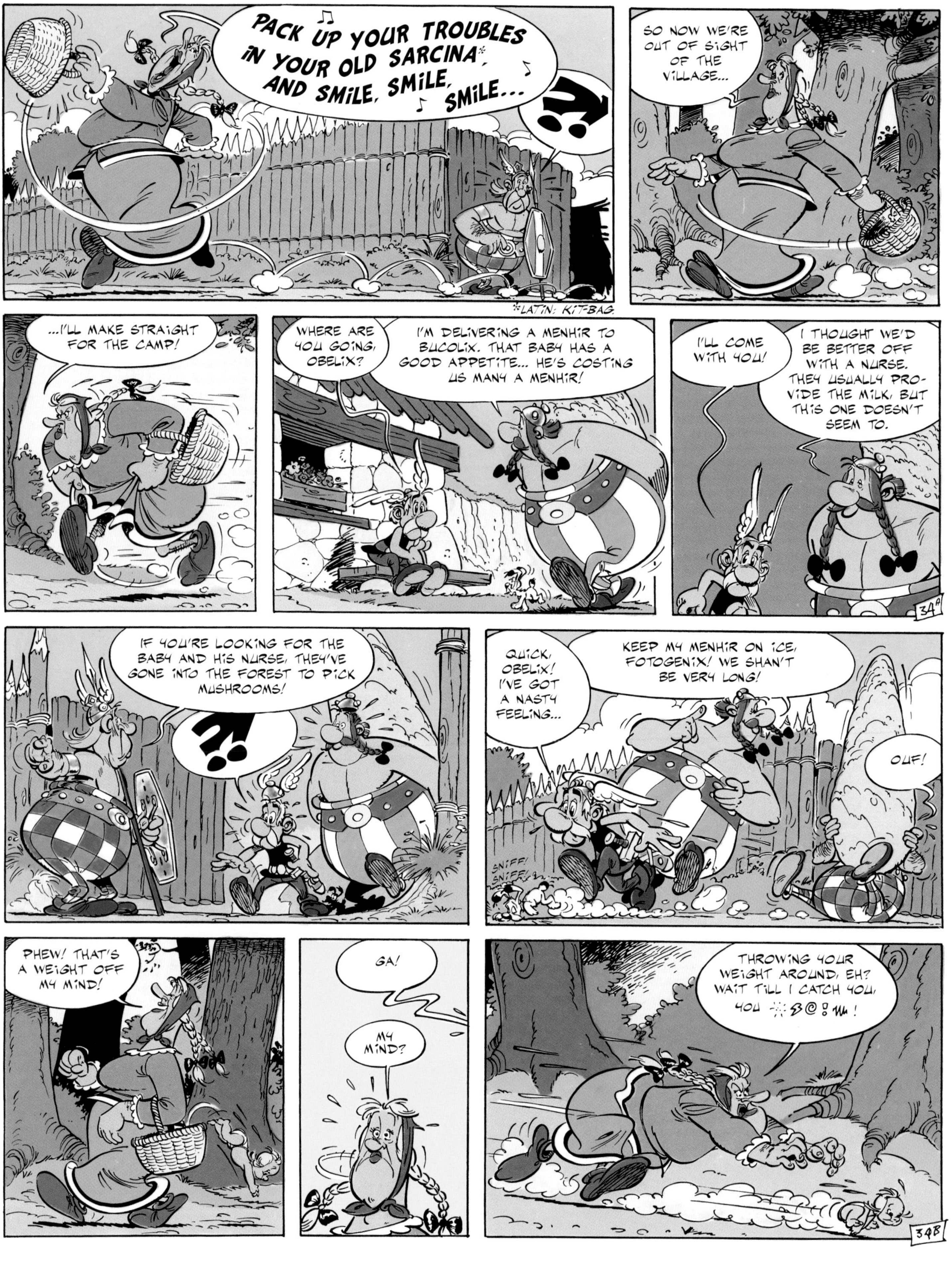
PACK UP YOUR TROUBLES IN YOUR OLD SARCINA*, AND SMILE, SMILE, SMILE...
?!
*LATIN: KIT-BAG.
SO NOW WE'RE OUT OF SIGHT OF THE VILLAGE...
...I'LL MAKE STRAIGHT FOR THE CAMP!
WHERE ARE YOU GOING, OBELIX?
I'M DELIVERING A MENHIR TO BUCOLIX. THAT BABY HAS A GOOD APPETITE... HE'S COSTING US MANY A MENHIR!
I'LL COME WITH YOU!
I THOUGHT WE'D BE BETTER OFF WITH A NURSE. THEY USUALLY PROVIDE THE MILK, BUT THIS ONE DOESN'T SEEM TO.
34A
IF YOU'RE LOOKING FOR THE BABY AND HIS NURSE, THEY'VE GONE INTO THE FOREST TO PICK MUSHROOMS!
?!
QUICK, OBELIX! I'VE GOT A NASTY FEELING...
KEEP MY MENHIR ON ICE, FOTOGENIX! WE SHAN'T BE VERY LONG!
OUF!
SNIFF! SNIFF!
PHEW! THAT'S A WEIGHT OFF MY MIND!
GA!
MY MIND?
!
THROWING YOUR WEIGHT AROUND, EH? WAIT TILL I CATCH YOU, YOU ☼✻@!!
34B

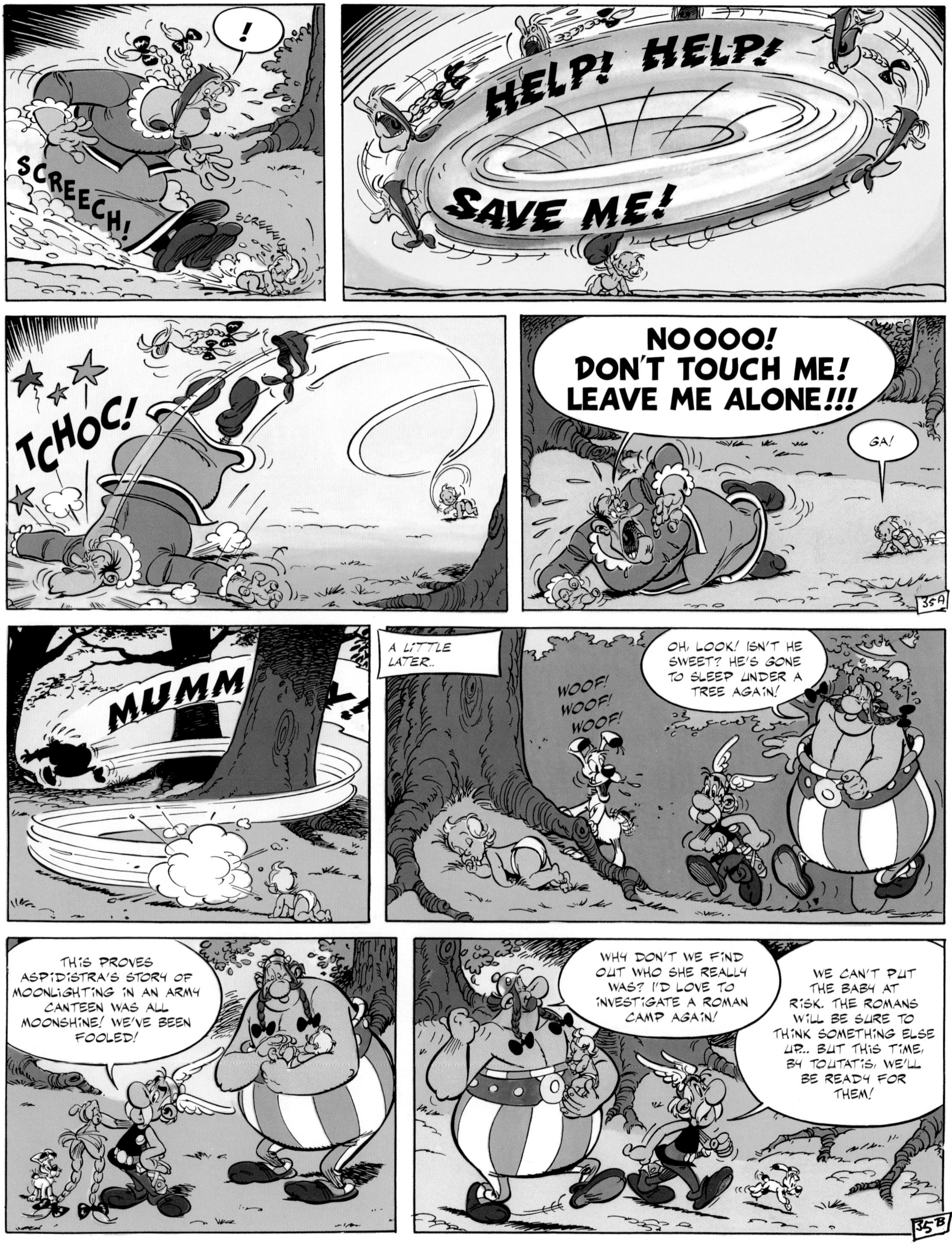
!
SCREECH!
SCREEEECH
HELP! HELP!
SAVE ME!
TCHOC!
NOOOO! DON'T TOUCH ME! LEAVE ME ALONE!!!
GA!
35A
MUMM
A LITTLE LATER..
WOOF! WOOF! WOOF!
OH, LOOK! ISN'T HE SWEET? HE'S GONE TO SLEEP UNDER A TREE AGAIN!
THIS PROVES ASPIDISTRA'S STORY OF MOONLIGHTING IN AN ARMY CANTEEN WAS ALL MOONSHINE! WE'VE BEEN FOOLED!
WHY DON'T WE FIND OUT WHO SHE REALLY WAS? I'D LOVE TO INVESTIGATE A ROMAN CAMP AGAIN!
WE CAN'T PUT THE BABY AT RISK. THE ROMANS WILL BE SURE TO THINK SOMETHING ELSE UP.. BUT THIS TIME, BY TOUTATIS, WE'LL BE READY FOR THEM!
35B

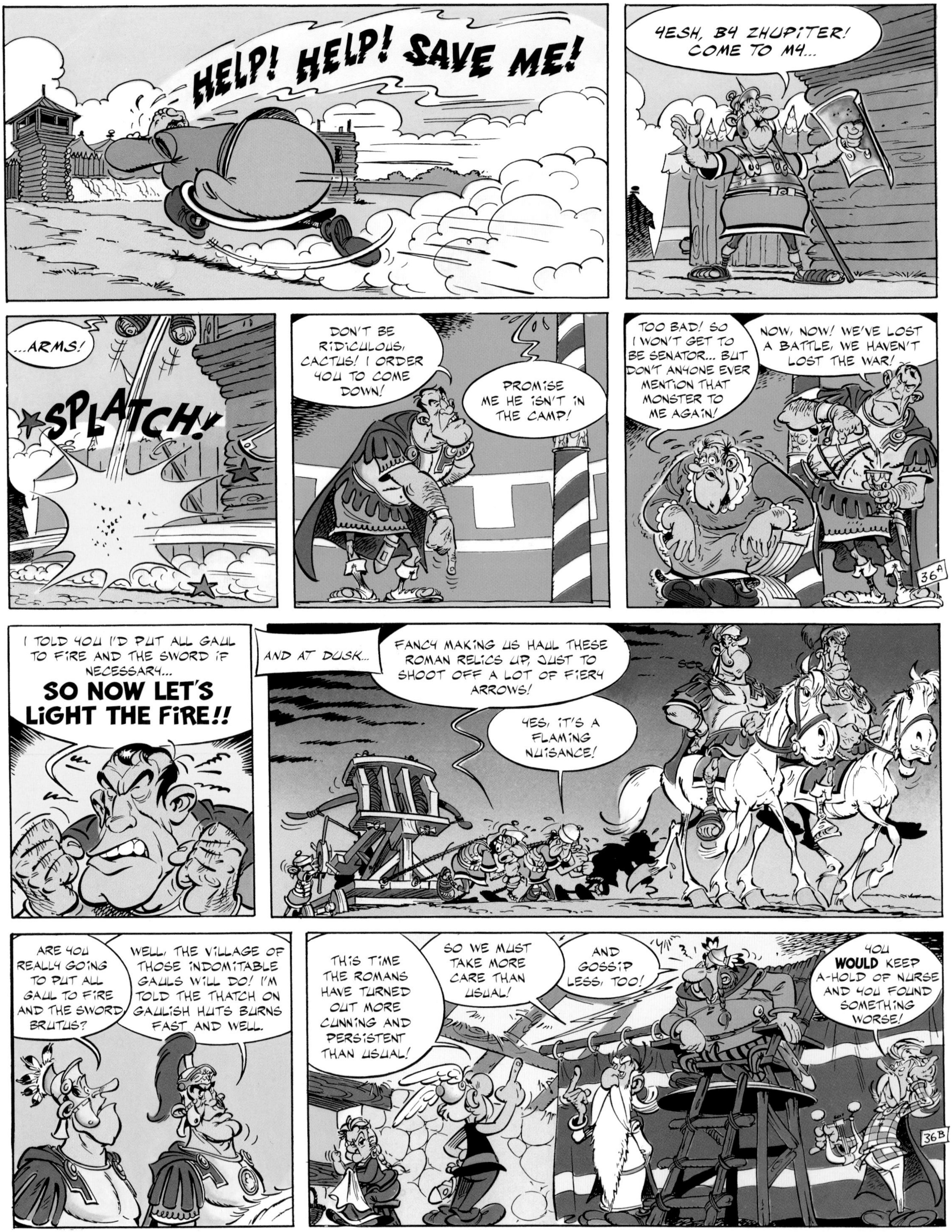
HELP! HELP! SAVE ME!
YESH, BY ZHUPITER! COME TO MY...
...ARMS!
SPLATCH!
DON'T BE RIDICULOUS, CACTUS! I ORDER YOU TO COME DOWN!
PROMISE ME HE ISN'T IN THE CAMP!
TOO BAD! SO I WON'T GET TO BE SENATOR... BUT DON'T ANYONE EVER MENTION THAT MONSTER TO ME AGAIN!
NOW, NOW! WE'VE LOST A BATTLE, WE HAVEN'T LOST THE WAR!
36A
I TOLD YOU I'D PUT ALL GAUL TO FIRE AND THE SWORD IF NECESSARY...
SO NOW LET'S LIGHT THE FIRE!!
AND AT DUSK...
FANCY MAKING US HAUL THESE ROMAN RELICS UP, JUST TO SHOOT OFF A LOT OF FIERY ARROWS!
YES, IT'S A FLAMING NUISANCE!
ARE YOU REALLY GOING TO PUT ALL GAUL TO FIRE AND THE SWORD BRUTUS?
WELL, THE VILLAGE OF THOSE INDOMITABLE GAULS WILL DO! I'M TOLD THE THATCH ON GAULISH HUTS BURNS FAST AND WELL.
THIS TIME THE ROMANS HAVE TURNED OUT MORE CUNNING AND PERSISTENT THAN USUAL!
SO WE MUST TAKE MORE CARE THAN USUAL!
AND GOSSIP LESS, TOO!
YOU WOULD KEEP A-HOLD OF NURSE AND YOU FOUND SOMETHING WORSE!
36B

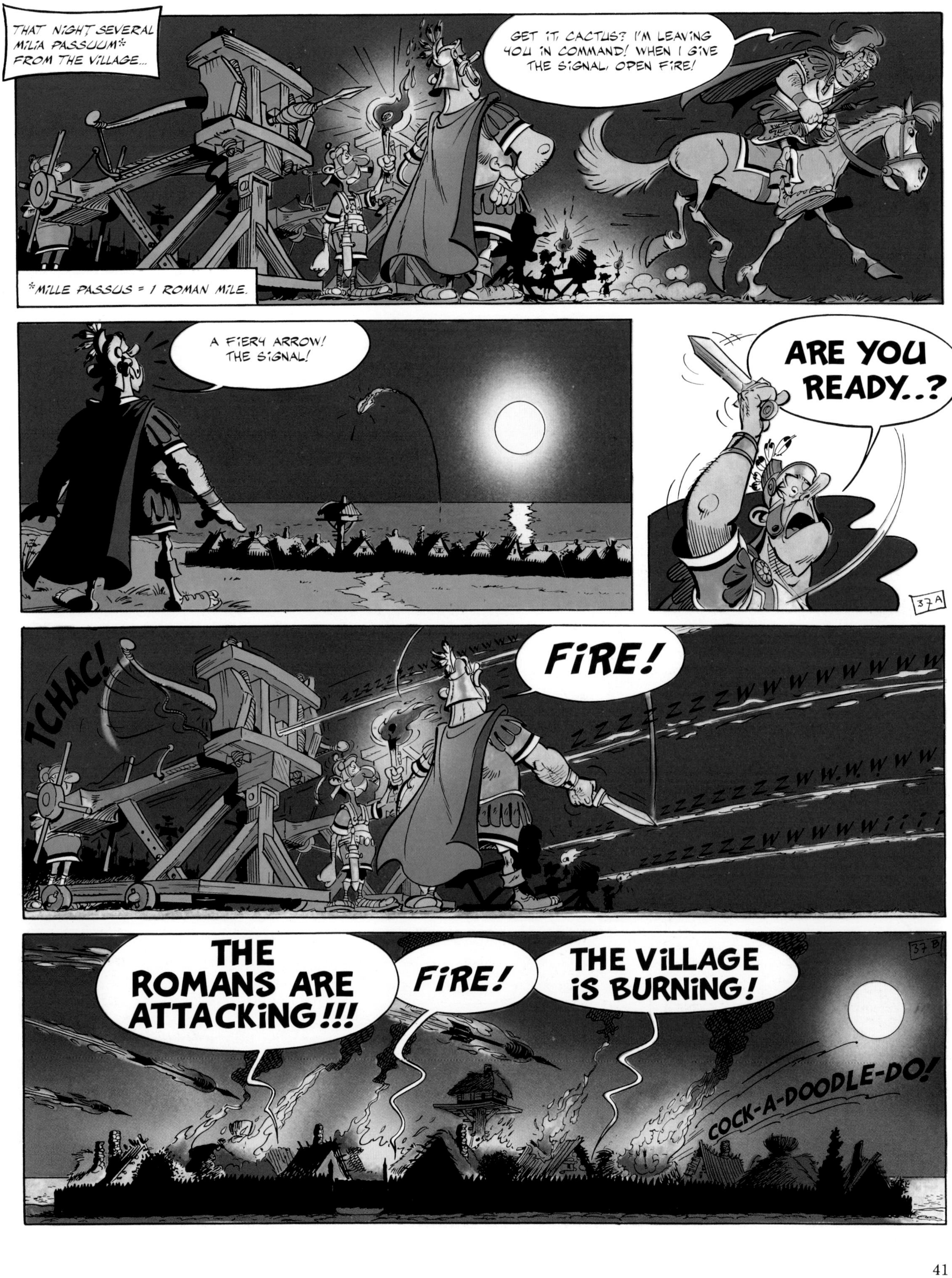
THAT NIGHT SEVERAL MILIA PASSUUM* FROM THE VILLAGE...
GET IT, CACTUS? I'M LEAVING YOU IN COMMAND! WHEN I GIVE THE SIGNAL, OPEN FIRE!
*MILLE PASSUS = 1 ROMAN MILE.
A FIERY ARROW! THE SIGNAL!
ARE YOU READY..?
37A
TCHAC!
FIRE!
37B
THE ROMANS ARE ATTACKING!!!
FIRE!
THE VILLAGE IS BURNING!
COCK-A-DOODLE-DO!

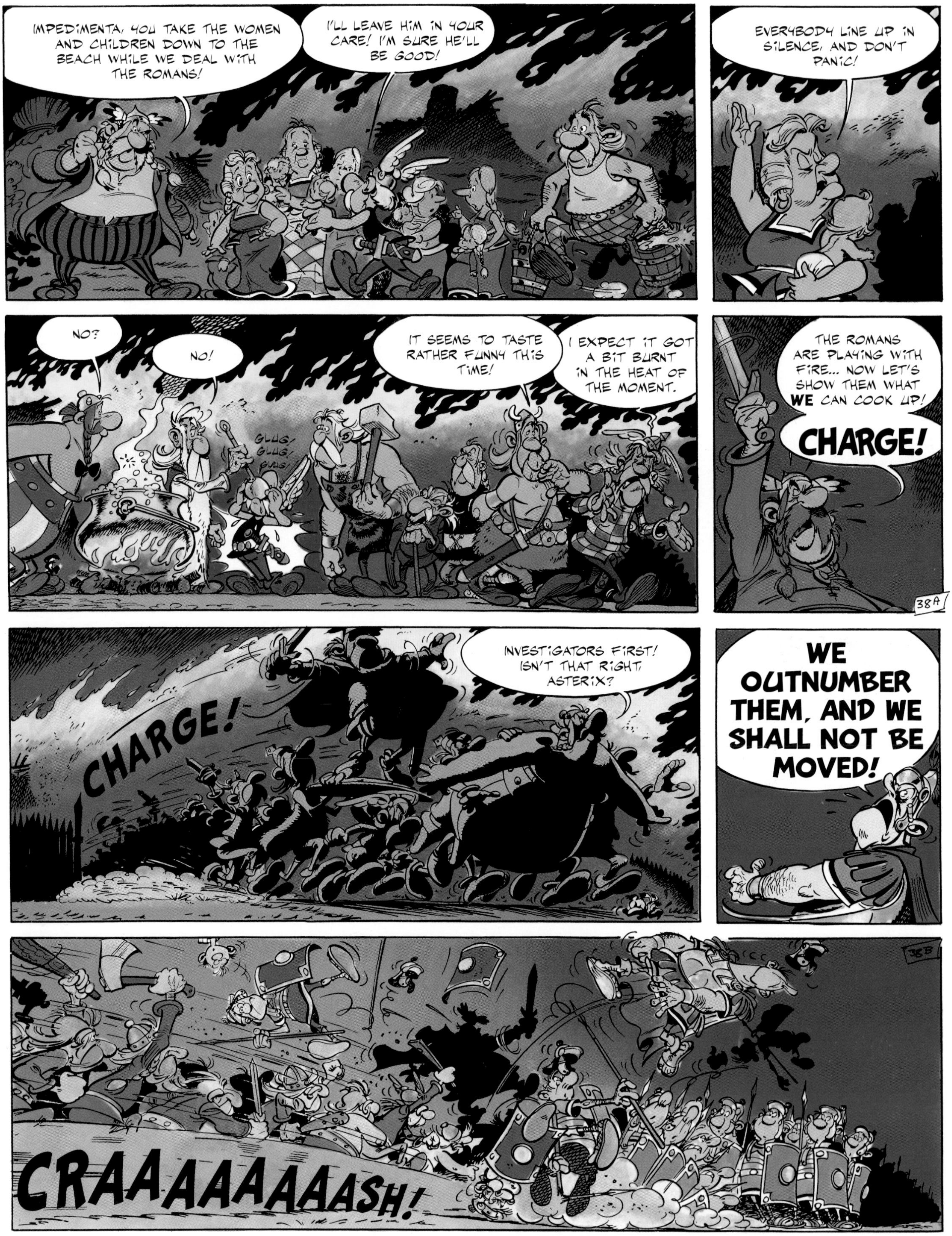

IMPEDIMENTA, YOU TAKE THE WOMEN AND CHILDREN DOWN TO THE BEACH WHILE WE DEAL WITH THE ROMANS!
I'LL LEAVE HIM IN YOUR CARE! I'M SURE HE'LL BE GOOD!
EVERYBODY LINE UP IN SILENCE, AND DON'T PANIC!
NO?
NO!
GLUG, GLUG, GLUG!
IT SEEMS TO TASTE RATHER FUNNY THIS TIME!
I EXPECT IT GOT A BIT BURNT IN THE HEAT OF THE MOMENT.
THE ROMANS ARE PLAYING WITH FIRE... NOW LET'S SHOW THEM WHAT WE CAN COOK UP!
CHARGE!
38A
CHARGE!
INVESTIGATORS FIRST! ISN'T THAT RIGHT, ASTERIX?
WE OUTNUMBER THEM, AND WE SHALL NOT BE MOVED!
38B
CRAAAAAAAAASH!

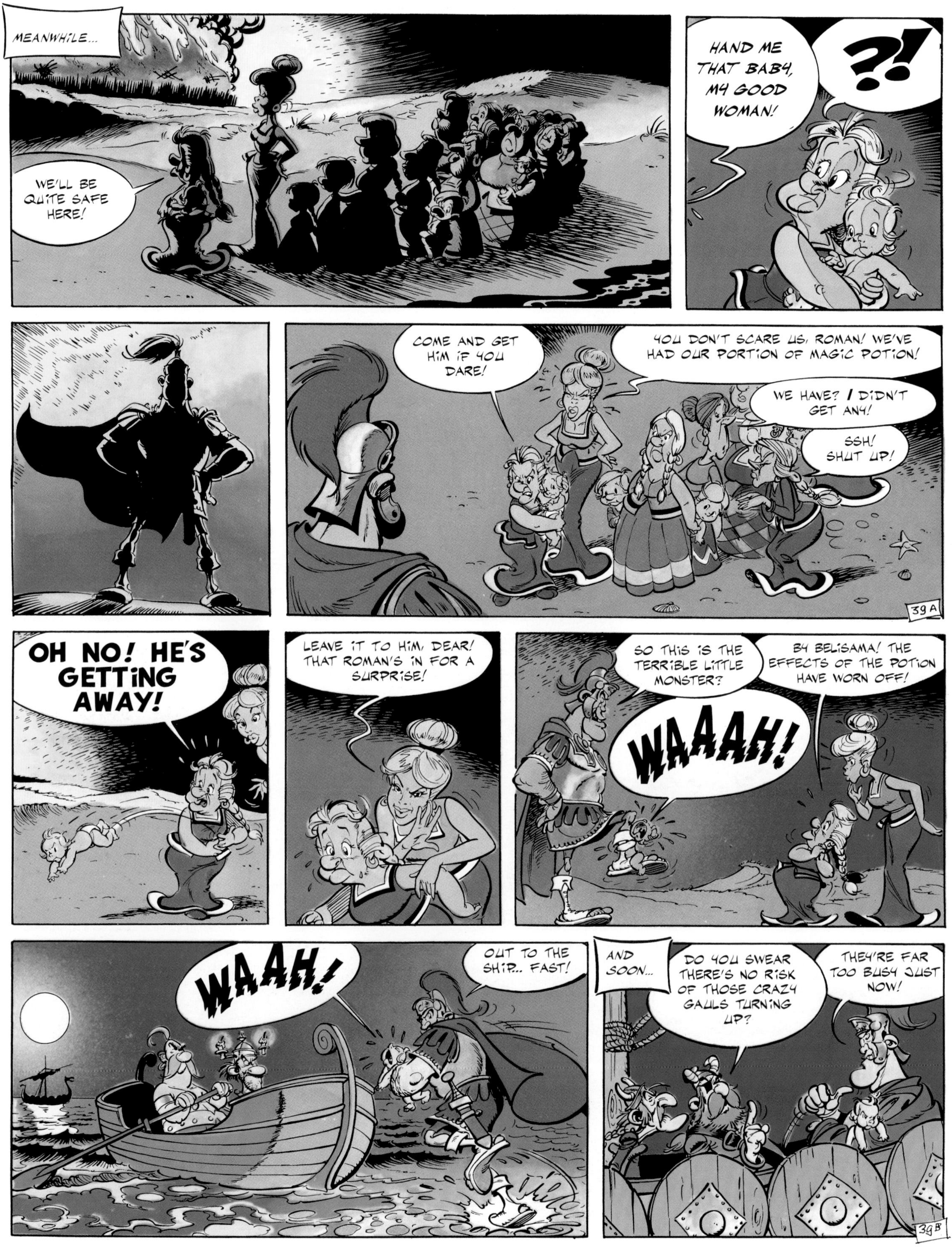
MEANWHILE...
WE'LL BE QUITE SAFE HERE!
HAND ME THAT BABY, MY GOOD WOMAN!
?!
COME AND GET HIM IF YOU DARE!
YOU DON'T SCARE US, ROMAN! WE'VE HAD OUR PORTION OF MAGIC POTION!
WE HAVE? I DIDN'T GET ANY!
SSH! SHUT UP!
39 A
OH NO! HE'S GETTING AWAY!
LEAVE IT TO HIM, DEAR! THAT ROMAN'S IN FOR A SURPRISE!
SO THIS IS THE TERRIBLE LITTLE MONSTER?
WAAAH!
BY BELISAMA! THE EFFECTS OF THE POTION HAVE WORN OFF!
WAAH!
OUT TO THE SHIP.. FAST!
AND SOON...
DO YOU SWEAR THERE'S NO RISK OF THOSE CRAZY GAULS TURNING UP?
THEY'RE FAR TOO BUSY JUST NOW!
39 B

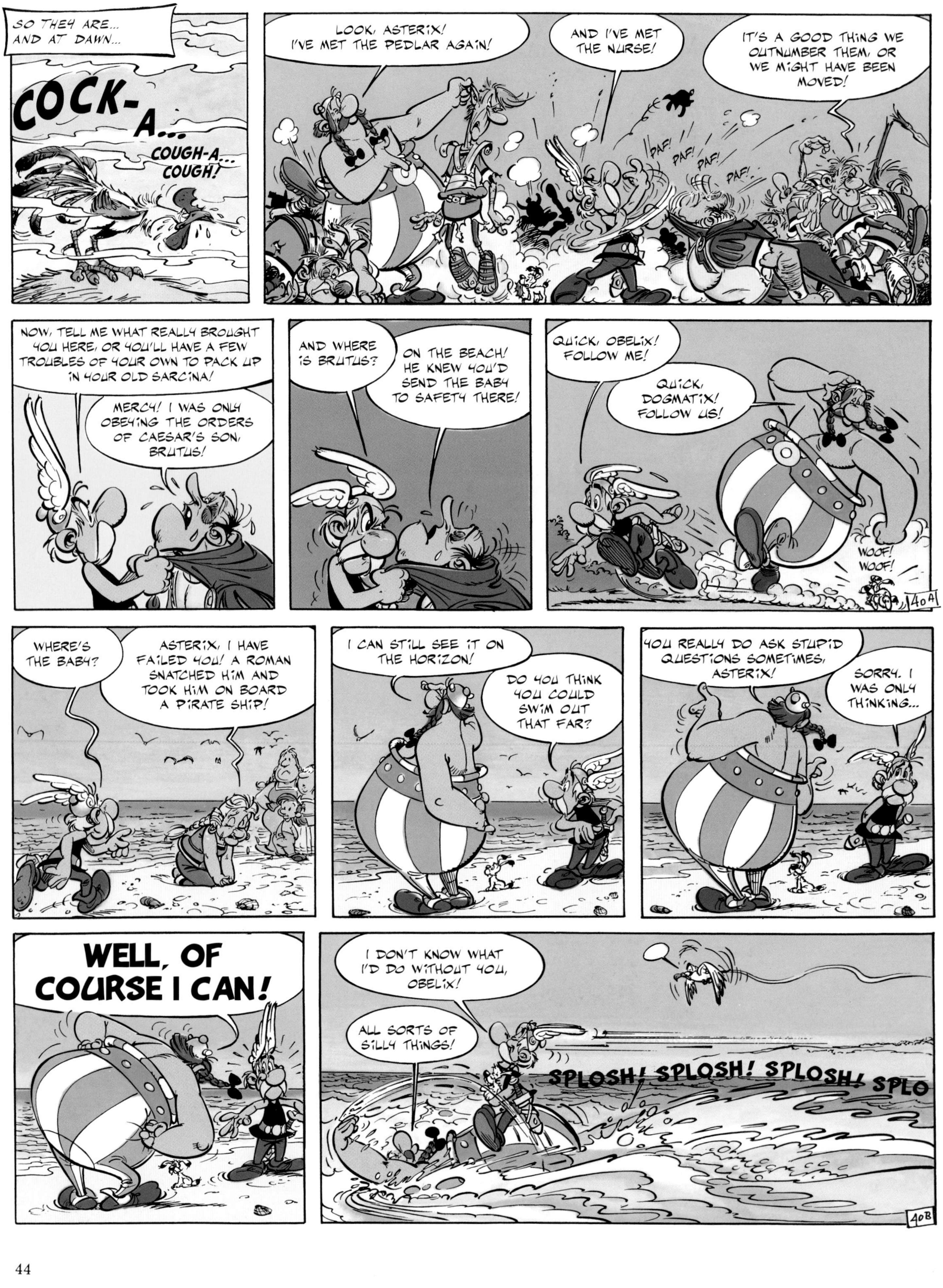

SO THEY ARE... AND AT DAWN...
COCK-A...
COUGH-A... COUGH!
LOOK, ASTERIX! I'VE MET THE PEDLAR AGAIN!
AND I'VE MET THE NURSE!
IT'S A GOOD THING WE OUTNUMBER THEM, OR WE MIGHT HAVE BEEN MOVED!
PAF! PAF! PAF! PAF!
NOW, TELL ME WHAT REALLY BROUGHT YOU HERE, OR YOU'LL HAVE A FEW TROUBLES OF YOUR OWN TO PACK UP IN YOUR OLD SARCINA!
MERCY! I WAS ONLY OBEYING THE ORDERS OF CAESAR'S SON, BRUTUS!
AND WHERE IS BRUTUS?
ON THE BEACH! HE KNEW YOU'D SEND THE BABY TO SAFETY THERE!
QUICK, OBELIX! FOLLOW ME!
QUICK, DOGMATIX! FOLLOW US!
WOOF! WOOF!
40A
WHERE'S THE BABY?
ASTERIX, I HAVE FAILED YOU! A ROMAN SNATCHED HIM AND TOOK HIM ON BOARD A PIRATE SHIP!
I CAN STILL SEE IT ON THE HORIZON!
DO YOU THINK YOU COULD SWIM OUT THAT FAR?
YOU REALLY DO ASK STUPID QUESTIONS SOMETIMES, ASTERIX!
SORRY. I WAS ONLY THINKING...
WELL, OF COURSE I CAN!
I DON'T KNOW WHAT I'D DO WITHOUT YOU, OBELIX!
ALL SORTS OF SILLY THINGS!
SPLOSH! SPLOSH! SPLOSH! SPLO
40B

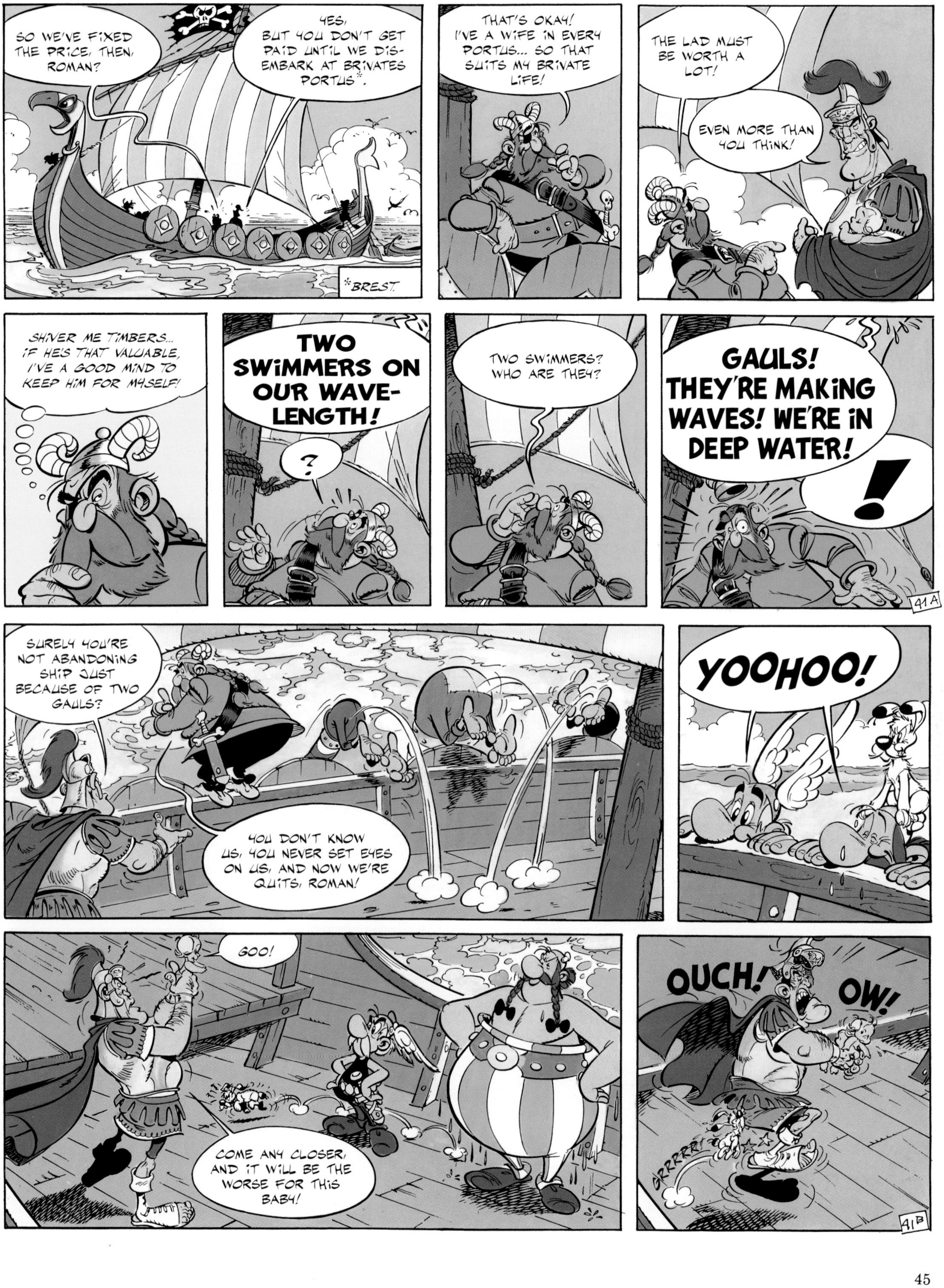

SO WE'VE FIXED THE PRICE, THEN, ROMAN?
YES, BUT YOU DON'T GET PAID UNTIL WE DISEMBARK AT BRIVATES PORTUS*.
*BREST.
THAT'S OKAY! I'VE A WIFE IN EVERY PORTUS... SO THAT SUITS MY BRIVATE LIFE!
THE LAD MUST BE WORTH A LOT!
EVEN MORE THAN YOU THINK!
SHIVER ME TIMBERS... IF HE'S THAT VALUABLE, I'VE A GOOD MIND TO KEEP HIM FOR MYSELF!
TWO SWIMMERS ON OUR WAVE-LENGTH!
?
TWO SWIMMERS? WHO ARE THEY?
GAULS! THEY'RE MAKING WAVES! WE'RE IN DEEP WATER!
!
41A
SURELY YOU'RE NOT ABANDONING SHIP JUST BECAUSE OF TWO GAULS?
YOU DON'T KNOW US, YOU NEVER SET EYES ON US, AND NOW WE'RE QUITS, ROMAN!
YOOHOO!
GOO!
COME ANY CLOSER, AND IT WILL BE THE WORSE FOR THIS BABY!
OUCH!
OW!
GRRRRR!
41B

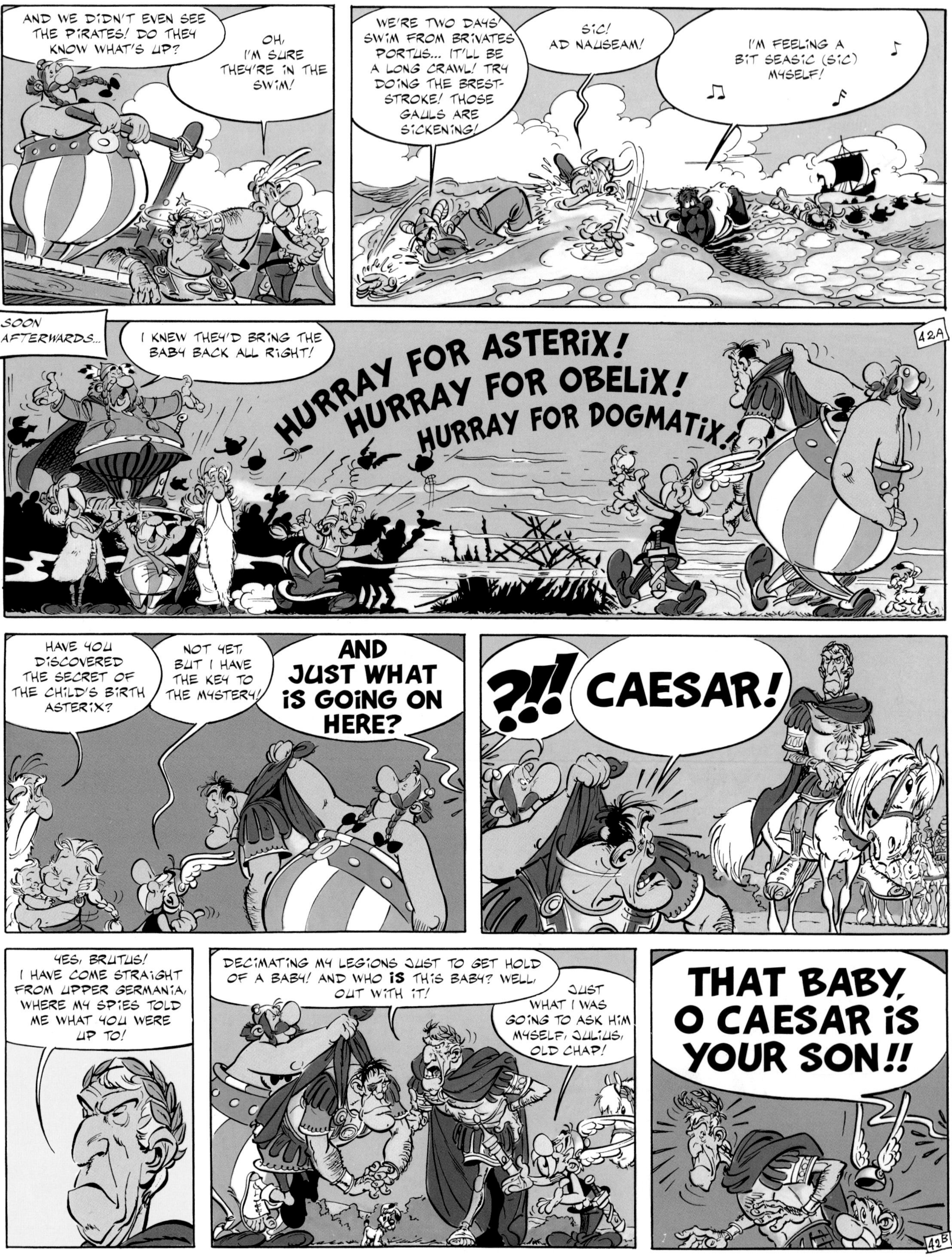
AND WE DIDN'T EVEN SEE THE PIRATES! DO THEY KNOW WHAT'S UP?
OH, I'M SURE THEY'RE IN THE SWIM!
WE'RE TWO DAYS' SWIM FROM BRIVATES PORTUS... IT'LL BE A LONG CRAWL! TRY DOING THE BREST-STROKE! THOSE GAULS ARE SICKENING!
SIC! AD NAUSEAM!
I'M FEELING A BIT SEASIC (SIC) MYSELF!
SOON AFTERWARDS...
I KNEW THEY'D BRING THE BABY BACK ALL RIGHT!
42A
HURRAY FOR ASTERIX!
HURRAY FOR OBELIX!
HURRAY FOR DOGMATIX!
HAVE YOU DISCOVERED THE SECRET OF THE CHILD'S BIRTH ASTERIX?
NOT YET, BUT I HAVE THE KEY TO THE MYSTERY!
AND JUST WHAT IS GOING ON HERE?
?!!
CAESAR!
YES, BRUTUS! I HAVE COME STRAIGHT FROM UPPER GERMANIA, WHERE MY SPIES TOLD ME WHAT YOU WERE UP TO!
DECIMATING MY LEGIONS JUST TO GET HOLD OF A BABY! AND WHO IS THIS BABY? WELL, OUT WITH IT!
JUST WHAT I WAS GOING TO ASK HIM MYSELF, JULIUS, OLD CHAP!
THAT BABY, O CAESAR IS YOUR SON!!
42B

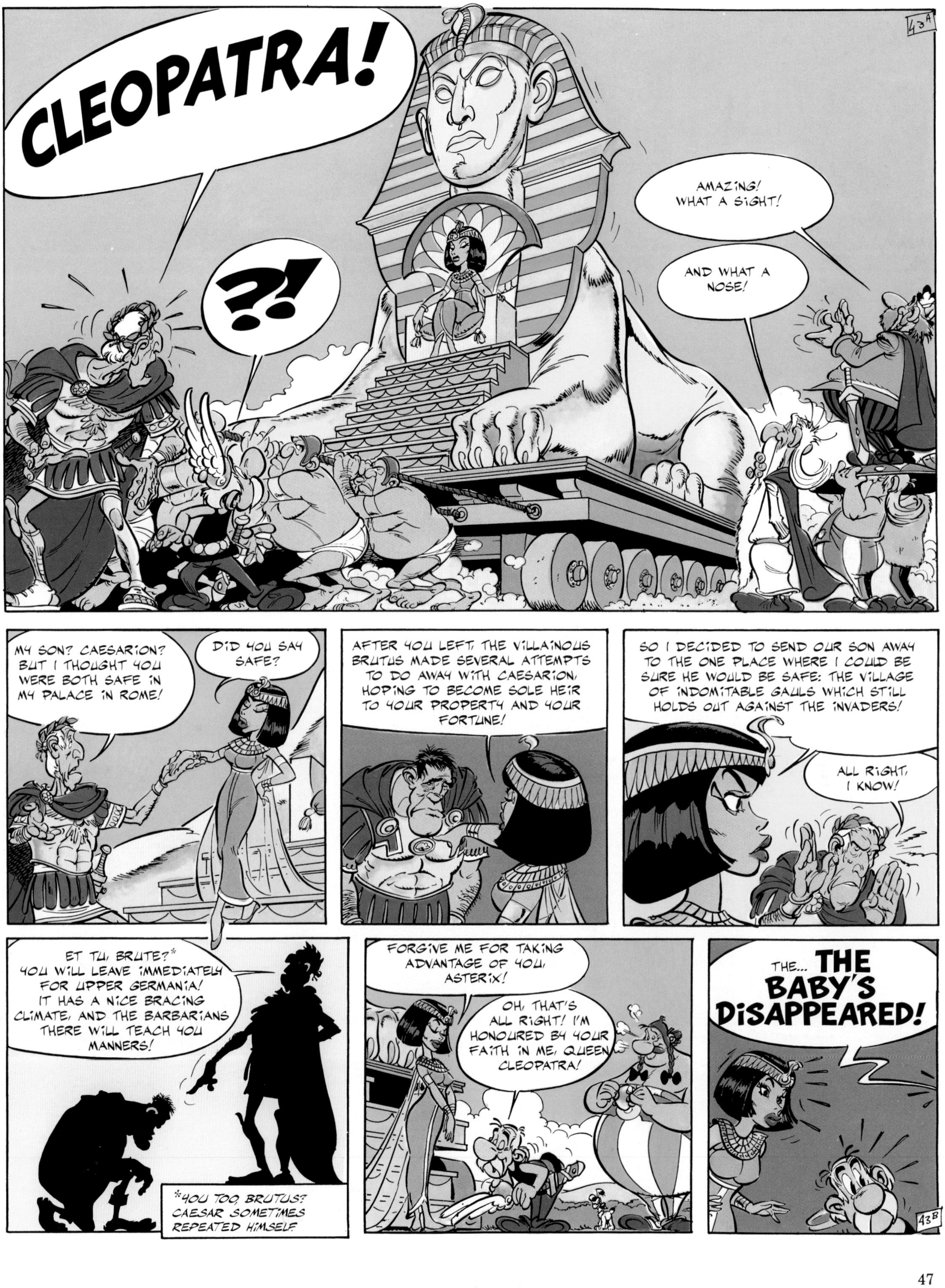
CLEOPATRA!
?!
AMAZING! WHAT A SIGHT!
AND WHAT A NOSE!
MY SON? CAESARION? BUT I THOUGHT YOU WERE BOTH SAFE IN MY PALACE IN ROME!
DID YOU SAY SAFE?
AFTER YOU LEFT, THE VILLAINOUS BRUTUS MADE SEVERAL ATTEMPTS TO DO AWAY WITH CAESARION, HOPING TO BECOME SOLE HEIR TO YOUR PROPERTY AND YOUR FORTUNE!
SO I DECIDED TO SEND OUR SON AWAY TO THE ONE PLACE WHERE I COULD BE SURE HE WOULD BE SAFE: THE VILLAGE OF INDOMITABLE GAULS WHICH STILL HOLDS OUT AGAINST THE INVADERS!
ALL RIGHT, I KNOW!
ET TU, BRUTE?* YOU WILL LEAVE IMMEDIATELY FOR UPPER GERMANIA! IT HAS A NICE BRACING CLIMATE, AND THE BARBARIANS THERE WILL TEACH YOU MANNERS!
*YOU TOO, BRUTUS? CAESAR SOMETIMES REPEATED HIMSELF.
FORGIVE ME FOR TAKING ADVANTAGE OF YOU, ASTERIX!
OH, THAT'S ALL RIGHT! I'M HONOURED BY YOUR FAITH IN ME, QUEEN CLEOPATRA!
THE... THE BABY'S DISAPPEARED!

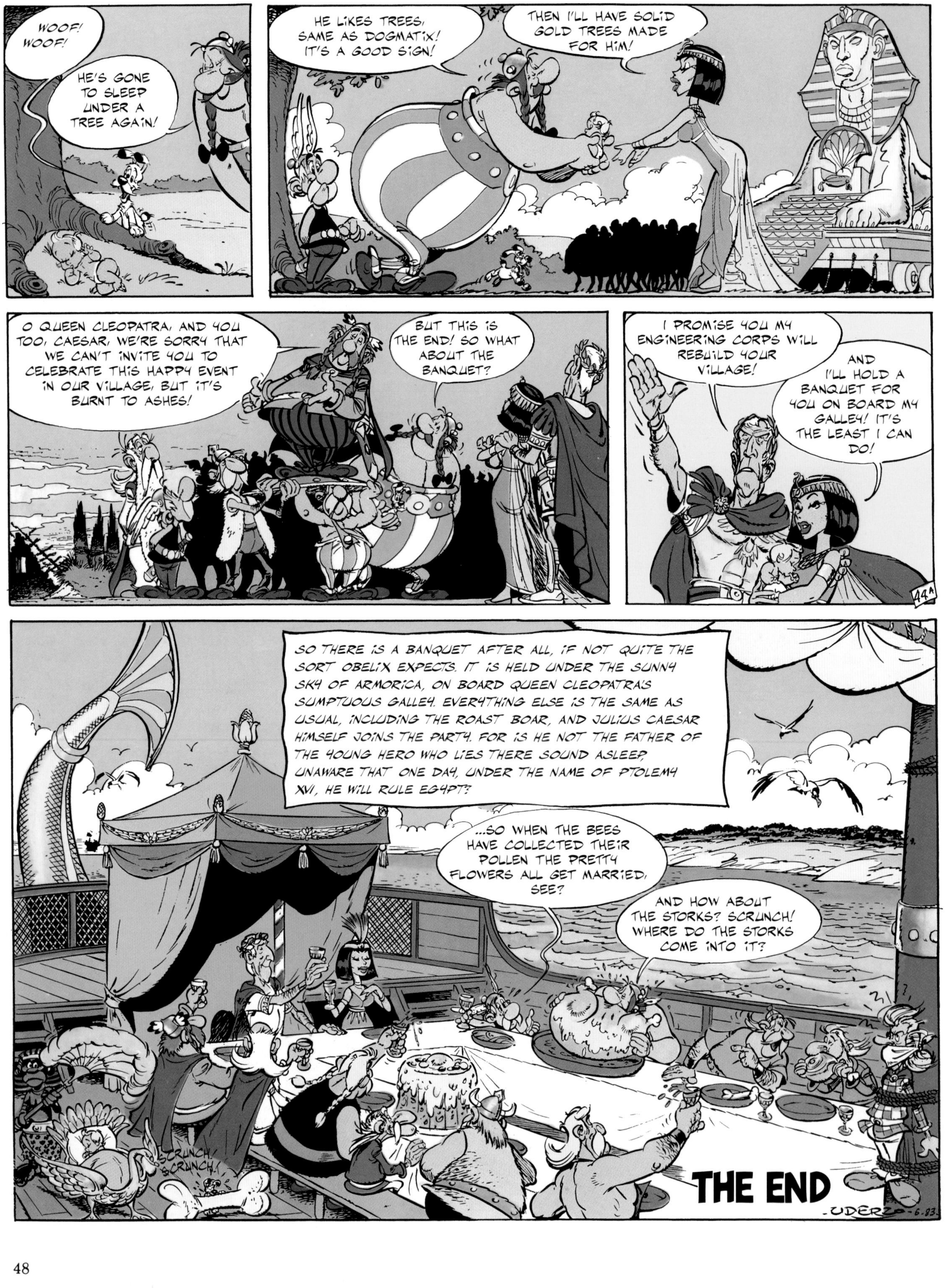
WOOF! WOOF!
HE'S GONE TO SLEEP UNDER A TREE AGAIN!
HE LIKES TREES, SAME AS DOGMATIX! IT'S A GOOD SIGN!
THEN I'LL HAVE SOLID GOLD TREES MADE FOR HIM!
O QUEEN CLEOPATRA, AND YOU TOO, CAESAR, WE'RE SORRY THAT WE CAN'T INVITE YOU TO CELEBRATE THIS HAPPY EVENT IN OUR VILLAGE, BUT IT'S BURNT TO ASHES!
BUT THIS IS THE END! SO WHAT ABOUT THE BANQUET?
I PROMISE YOU MY ENGINEERING CORPS WILL REBUILD YOUR VILLAGE!
AND I'LL HOLD A BANQUET FOR YOU ON BOARD MY GALLEY! IT'S THE LEAST I CAN DO!
44A
SO THERE IS A BANQUET AFTER ALL, IF NOT QUITE THE SORT OBELIX EXPECTS. IT IS HELD UNDER THE SUNNY SKY OF ARMORICA, ON BOARD QUEEN CLEOPATRA'S SUMPTUOUS GALLEY. EVERYTHING ELSE IS THE SAME AS USUAL, INCLUDING THE ROAST BOAR, AND JULIUS CAESAR HIMSELF JOINS THE PARTY. FOR IS HE NOT THE FATHER OF THE YOUNG HERO WHO LIES THERE SOUND ASLEEP, UNAWARE THAT ONE DAY, UNDER THE NAME OF PTOLEMY XVI, HE WILL RULE EGYPT?
...SO WHEN THE BEES HAVE COLLECTED THEIR POLLEN THE PRETTY FLOWERS ALL GET MARRIED, SEE?
AND HOW ABOUT THE STORKS? SCRUNCH! WHERE DO THE STORKS COME INTO IT?
SCRUNCH! SCRUNCH!
THE END
UDERZO 6.83

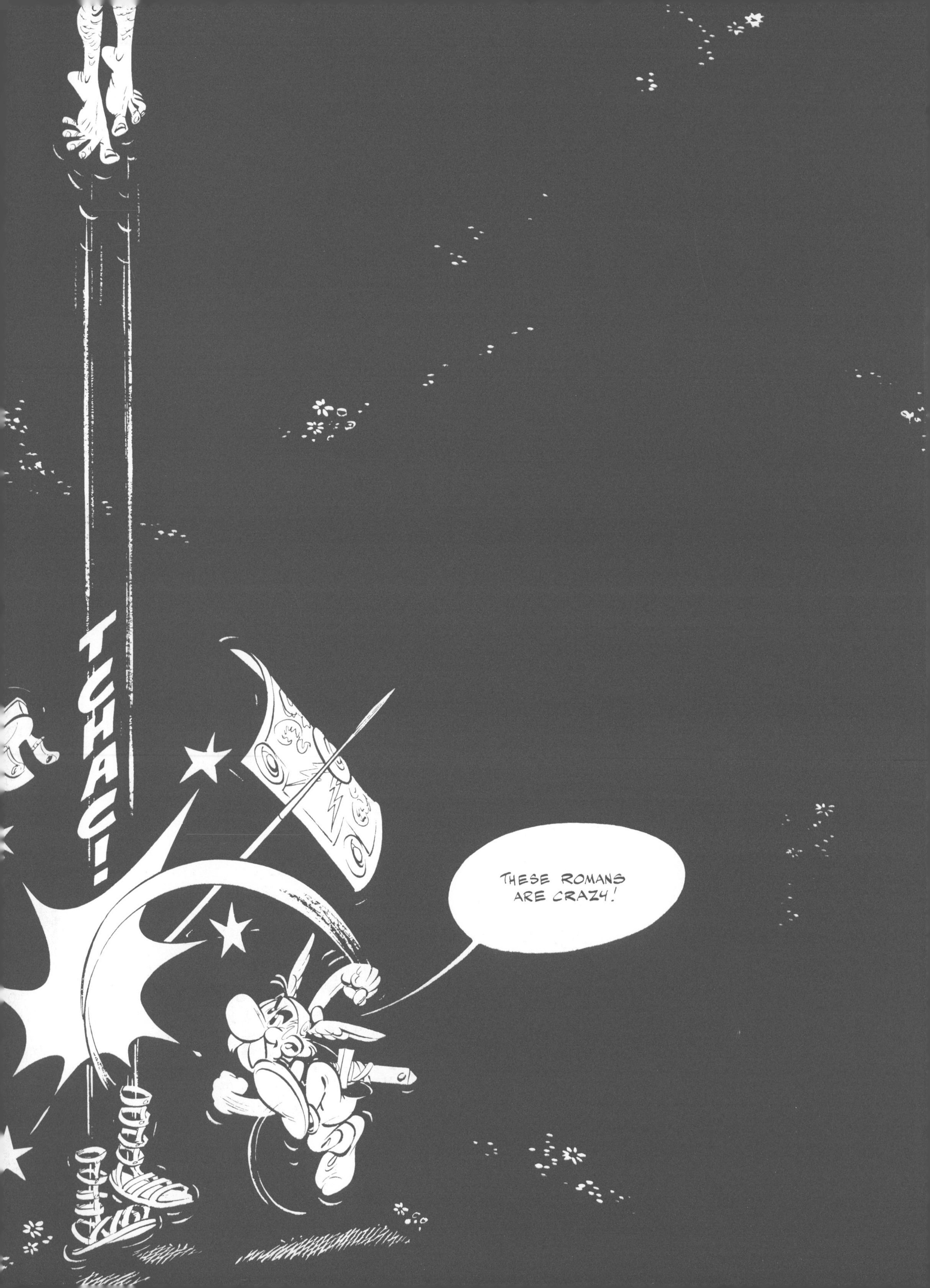

TCHAC!!
THESE ROMANS ARE CRAZY!